Tacenda Literary Magazine

2014 Edition

EDITORS-IN-CHIEF
Alexa Marie Kelly
Hannah Ehlers

CONSULTING EDITOR
Robert Johnson

COVER DESIGN
Carla Mavaddat

TEXT DESIGN
Sonia Tabriz

BleakHouse Publishing
2014

Ward Circle Building 254
American University
Washington, DC 20016

NEC Box 67
New England College
Henniker, New Hampshire 03242
www.BleakHousePublishing.com

Robert Johnson – Editor & Publisher
Sonia Tabriz - Managing Editor
Liz Calka - Art Director

Rachel Cupelo - Marketing Director
Shirin Karimi - Senior Creative Consultant
Carla Mavaddat - Curator

Joanna Heaney – Chief Operating Officer
Alexa Marie Kelly – Chief Editorial Officer
Nora Kirk – Chief Development Officer
Rachel Ternes – Chief Creative Officer

Copyright © 2014 by Robert Johnson

ISBN: 978-0-9837769-8-7

Printed in the United States of America

A Note From the Editors

TACENDA: n., pronounced ta'KEN'da
'things better left unsaid'

BleakHouse may have a misleading name. Our writers sing from the darker corners of humanity, but that does not make them dark. Their light shines outward through their art. We want to see their light, their songs, their stories. Even if their stories are bleak.

We publish Tacenda Literary Magazine not to celebrate what's bleak but to expose it, so that we can foster hope for the future. Each page of Tacenda 2014 exposes our criminal justice system. Some of our authors have been entangled in the system. Some are still in prison. All of our artists have thought about the experience of men and women behind bars. The men and women we label criminals but often forget to label as human.

Tacenda recognizes humanity, its forms and disfigurements.

We are proud to present the most diverse collection of authors in the history of Tacenda. They come from all walks of life. Students. Prisoners. Writers. Photographers. Advocates. All people, passionate about justice.

Together, these great works of art and literature challenge popular notions of crime. They shed light on what it means to be a prisoner, and ultimately, what it means to be human.

Thank you to our writers, especially those writing from prison cells (real or in our hearts and minds.) Thank you to Professor Robert Johnson, our consulting editor and mentor. You inspire us. You forgive and encourage everyone you know.

Thank you reader for your continued support and open mind.

Alexa Marie Kelly
Hannah Ehlers
Editors-in-Chief

Table of Contents

II. Short Stories

III. Essays

IV. Plays

V. Photography

POETRY

Choosing Experience
Stephanie Vela

Don't tell me to choose to be sympathetic and
understanding. Don't tell me to choose to be cold and
uncaring. It's hard to choose when experience beckons
you.

See, you know what you've been through, and you
wouldn't believe the hell that we've been through

Let me start with a story. Just one or two
Look over. Heavy Breathing.
Baggy Pants, cortezes, white shirt.
Heart beating, beating, breaking, LITERALLY I think
my heart is breaking.
Dragged out the car.
Gun to the head.
Life Flashing.
CLICK.
Exhale, thank God, I'm alive.

Hands touching me
Raped.
He's faded, it's okay.
Years later.
He's Overdosed.
Dead.
You can't touch me that way

This man, an uncle, closer than a friend

I'm not kidding you, you really wouldn't believe the hell
we've been through

The gangs, the crazies of the street
Driveby.
You better DUCK!
Friend shot once.
Look over, there's blood.
Ambulances, sirens, no justice in that gun,

Sixteen, the shooter's, just sixteen.

Car stopped for no reason.
Policeman walks.
Stares at me, glares at him.
Handcuffed on the side of the road. Criminals. I think. I
look like a damn criminal.
Let go. No ticket No fine. Just a nod and a pass.
Discrimination. Hell yes, it's still alive.

Homeless. Two weeks. House sold. Nowhere to go.
Staying on a neighbor's floor.
Domestic abuse.
A place like this, you close your eyes and that darkness is
better

You really, really can't picture this can you?

Gangs.
Bullet to the head.

Hands touching me
Rape
Drugs
Overdose
Death

Arrested
Separated

Scum
Immigrant
Discrimination

Poverty
Hunger
Nothing

Snitch.
Knife to throat
Beheaded.

See, Don't tell me to choose. Because you, you don't
know what I've been through.

Just Games
Cassandra Fowler

Tonight we will play a game
Team Johnson vs. Team USA
Winner takes all?

Tonight we will play our parts.
Two weeping mothers,
Three innocent bystanders,
One hero-uncast.
How shall we paint this backdrop?

Tonight we will play a tune
In dexterous hands, even the crudest instrument play
sweetly
Crash the cymbals.
Shock the audience.

Perhaps tomorrow we will realize that we wrote the rules
The next day we may rewrite them.

Perhaps the following morning we will realize that we live
the parts
The day after that we may eliminate the stage.

Perhaps one day we will stop singing and stop expecting
music,
Then, maybe there's a chance, we may speak and be
heard.

If I Walked with You
Cassandra Fowler

If I walked with you

Would my feet bleed,
Gashed by the glass you left broken on the ground?
Do your feet bleed now?

Would I drown in the deluge of sweat rushing from my
pores?
Would others drown too?

Would puss-filled bubbles push up to the surface of my
skin?
Would the heat of hellfire be too much too bear?
Is it too much for you?

And the rest of the condemned,
May I walk with them to?

I never wanted to be frigid,
And the cold hasn't yet numbed that memory,
But when you're numb you want nothing
And you are nothing, save an actor
And you pay no mind to the wants of others,
And you have no mind, you are lucky to move
And you are a glassy eyed,
With no soul behind the screen
And you become stoic
And you function properly.
You have been sculpted.

Does the devil sleep?
Yes he does, wrapped warmly in his grandmother's quilt.

I only fear that he dreams of me.

Blacks
Daniel Marks

Lined up,
Six packed.
He says, "You ready ma'am?"
I say "ok."

Dark skinned,
Du-ragged,
Baggy panted.
They all look the same.

Pistol pocketed
Ebonic prowess.
Justifiably locked up,
Stereotyped away.

It's him,
The darker one
Farthest left.
"Are you sure?"
No, but I tell him "yes."

Florescent
Emmy Cairns

Florescent I

The old church on the street corner has windows of
Tiffany glass. They were so precious that the windows
were blocked from the outside, shielded by plywood and
iron bars. The only light that shone through was artificial.
And I always thought it was the most beautiful thing I've
ever seen until the florescent in the hall pierced through
the bars of my cell and I was allowed to walk out in it for
two hours every day.

Florescent II

They say angels are accompanied by lights and harps and
choirs. Mine is accompanied by a single telephone and a
pane of glass.

Florescent III

I'm still waiting for the light they say you see right before
you die, but it will be just a broken, flickering florescent
over my crucifix.

Welcome to the World
Stephanie Vela

Welcome.
Welcome to the world. I hope you like it. It's fairly new.
Welcome to the world. Act like me, act like them and
you'll be fine I promise!
Where the land flows milk and honey, where the tastes
and the smells are without compare. Welcome to the
place where experience's cup is overflowing and all you
have to do is stretch your hand to get it. Yes! This is the
place!

But wait. Don't be a fool and mess this up. Because the
world will end for you. No more milk, no more honey.
Welcome to hell.

Revenge
Stephanie Vela

When a man performs an act of murder
Robbing the life of someone's love
We wish to greet him with the same favor
Giving him what we think he deserves

This way we think it's justified
Of course, we say, He HAD to die
Only then will yearning tears be dried
The hate and vengeance satisfied

That all that embedded bitterness
Antipathy and disgust
Will somehow diminish
The necessity for benevolence
All compassion and empathy
 Suddenly hushed

Just momentary insanity,
Just a lapse in humanity
We don't wish death on our own
But to hell with those who have killed
And left the rest of us to mourn

Eggs
Kristen Pulkstenis

I got up this morning and made eggs
Bacon with the crispy part and
toast like walking on fall leaves
with butter
because toast needs butter

And if I start a fire
by accident
They'll stop me from making eggs
Maybe someone else will make them for me

They stopped him from making eggs
Because he killed a man
Maybe it would work better if they stopped him
from killing a man instead

Absorbed Light
Valerie Rennoll

I had all these good intentions
Of blue and red and green.
And colorful combinations
Of magenta and cyan and yellow.
Pure, with a defined direction,
I was a white light.

But I was reflected,
And scattered along the way.
My colors absorbed one by one
Until this place took the last I had.
I am a muffled black [dark?] shadow
of blacks and greys.

All the light having been absorbed,
the only color we get here
is from the breaking of a shadow
to reveal the glowing drops
of vibrant red simmering
just beneath the indistinct outline.

Please Hold
Valerie Rennoll

I return a call to the doctor's office
Please hold, the doctor will be right with you.
Click.
Frustrating music.
Stuck until a tired clerk
Transfers me to the other line
Thirty seconds.
Two minutes.
Ten minutes.
Lost in line
They forget the life of mine
Waiting on the other side.

I answer questions for police officers.
Please hold, you are suspected of murder.
Click.
Handcuffs bind my hands.
Stuck until a tired judge
Decides what my future will be.
Thirty days.
Two months.
Ten years.
Lost in line
They forget the life of mine
Waiting on the other side.

Breathing in the Cosmos
Emma LoBuono

I am suspended in nothing.
I am not even myself,
just a stream of half-woken
consciousness
buoyed up by the cold that isn't meant
for someone once of the human race

The particles around me collide
as the key fits into the lock outside
and suddenly, I am hurtling
through the vacuum
as life floods in once more.

There is no wind in space
but my atoms whoosh back together
as I begin to reclaim myself
and the very first sun explodes
over the emptiness as the door opens
on cement blocks that stole the places
where rainbow nebulas
and spinning galaxies used to be.

A guard steps in
and the first faraway star
blinks into existence.
A planet forms below me,
a solid rock to pull me in
and break my fall.

My lungs are the first to form
and I breathe.
The cells of my body rush in

with every contraction of my lungs.
But I am still not yet me.
Inhale.
Exhale.

The atoms of these confining walls
slide into their place at the speed of light
and I am aware
of something besides blackness
and freezing. Winds start to rush
and fill my brand new ears.
I am close to impact.
Inhale.
Exhale.

Each breath I take makes me more solid.
I am real after all.
Existence pours into the void around me,
and billions upon billions of stars would blind me if my
eyes had already formed.
Inhale.
Exhale.

My fingers wiggle, my toes curl.
I regain myself, control creeping back in
as I am flung back together.
A hand closes around my newborn shoulder
and my unfinished body is yanked upwards.
Inhale.
Exhale.

I slam into the planet before I am ready,
forced out of solitude
and no longer suspended.
My legs aren't enough to hold myself up,
my electrons still struggling to find alignment.

Inhale.
Exhale.

The coldness of space is replaced
with the heat of reality
and it burns my raw skin, the flames
licking at me and blistering.
Inhale.
Exhale.

I stumble and my eyes fly open
and the first thing I see are
galaxies of dust motes flying from my lips
with every breath I take.
I inhale once more, a steadying breath,
and with the final exhale,
my own star winks back into existence.

Knee Jerk Reaction
Maggie Brennan

A mother in the back row tracks
her dear boy in the headlights
from holding to the front
of the courtroom to stand
to twitch
next to his appointed lawyer.

Numbers play off their tongues
case
prisoner
bail
shrouded in jargon she doesn't speak.
His face is impassive
his jaw pops down and his shoulder
springs up,
body convulsing.

The cops thought it was just some kind of
dope sick
just some kind of
off his meds
and reminded him with brutal thwumps that
twitching
was not permitted here.
You're gonna sit still so help me God.

A mother in the back row runs
dry fingers through dry hair
fighting back warrior cries
Just let them do their jobs
She breathed in the comfort that they knew
they had to know.

Bail: $2500
Was it battery or assault? She couldn't
remember through the
shocked
haze as it dawned on her that
they did not know.
maybe did not care.

There was only small comfort in
the thought that an
autistic boy
in this harsh system
at least wouldn't struggle
with averting
his
eyes.

Grading Tales from an Inner City Public School
Maggie Brennan

Does not play well with others
That's what you'd expect,
huh? I gotta be some sorta
psychopath, a problem
since the fucking
start.

Spelling and Grammar: D+

Inappropriate conduct in class.
It's funny, isn't it? That saying
"he hit me first" is a legitimate
defense in court but not a
classroom?

Attendance: F

I can't say a damn thing
bout that. School was a
drag and the high
was way better than
living through hell.

History: B

Shows promise when in class.
I loved that shit.
Reading that was like
watching Jerry Springer but
with funnier outfits.

Murder: C-

If there were teachers' notes
on that, they woulda said
something like:
Unprepared. No evident forethought.

(Revised)
Murder: F

For getting caught.
To Stay Human
Maggie Brennan

Questions are the currency
of the justice system.
Some people think it's
blood
others think it's
lies
But we trade questions
easy like filthy,
ancient coins.

Hey, man, how're things?
What did he do?
What the fuck do you think you're looking at?

But the one that always
trips me up
is the one she breathes through
miles of phone line.
Wire making her voice
sound broken.
Or maybe that's just the way
it really is.

I think about that question
now as I lift one hand
and scrape
my palm against the rough
of my cement walls.
The crimson turns brown
against dull gray
Fading instantly.

It should be evidence,
the clincher.
the answer
Do I not bleed?
But her words echo
in the muffle of
prison activity.

How do you do it? How do you
stay human?
And that's just it.
You don't.

Not For a Mother Like Me
Maggie Brennan

They say it's in the little moments of
awed stupor at a Disney flick or
the first drawing brought before
the cooing chorus of
"Well, baby, that's not bad!
Not bad at all."

But not for a mother like me.

She always held the crayons
too damn tight.
Smearing color across pages,
leaving pieces behind. And
other mothers gotta
to see the first time their kid
drew somebody and it looked
even remotely human.

But not for a mother like me.

Other mothers woulda
brought snacks in for birthdays
and let their crack pipe
wither in disuse. They woulda
been there for the walks home
and there woulda been
chatty smiles and small
warm hands waiting for them.

But not for a mother like me.

When I stare at the concrete of
my cell now I wonder if

her skin woulda been like this
Smooth but not perfect,
pockmarked with adolescence.
And other mothers get to see that,
I guess.

But not for a mother like me.

And I knew I shoulda paid
him and that we lived in a
world where punishment was
swift and outta hand.
Other mothers would look at
prom pictures or, hell, even
report cards. Not prison
bars and dead eyes.

But not for a mother like me.

I know there'll be teddy bears
propped under the stop sign
that she fell at, probably until
no one can remember that we
were supposed to have a
helluva lot more than
seven short years.
And other mothers get to see
wedding gowns and
arrogant boyfriends,
shining smiles and
rebellious eyeliner.

But not for a mother unchilded.

Not for a mother like me.

Ghosting Hands
Maggie Brennan

I.
I dip a foot off the edge
of my bed and let it swing
like a pirate from a noose,
the rough concrete floor scuffing
my sole raw.
I lay back and I can feel
ghosting hands,
memorized dreams. I run
through the motions,
the way he'd dance
fingertips up my forearm.
Distant now.
It's been sixteen years.

II.
She don't care about me,
hell, she don't know shit
about me. But this is her
job and as her pale,
ghosting hands
stretch diagnosis across
my bruised ribs
I think it's been
a helluva long time
since anyone touched me
that smooth and quiet.

III.
She's got all the COs
in her uniformed pocket,
the kind of woman where
you can almost still see

the hard bully on the
playground with a gossiped
past – did you hear what
her old man did
to her?
But that doesn't make much
difference when she's
ghosting hands up the
newbie's thighs,
soft skin trembling
from fear and
something else.

IV.
It's been too long
(Doesn't really matter how
long, cause six months and
six decades feel the same
without a hand to hold),
and I've forgotten.
I can feel the
ghosting hands
of old prisoners and
visitors and COs,
the dead,
but I can't remember
the pressure of
someone else's touch
dimpling my skin.
I can imagine
(and do I imagine!)
but I just can't
seem to
remember.

Black Bone
Alexa Marie Kelly

Tickets rain down
Like dead confetti.
Blue slips, court dates.
We slip, life waits.
We are the hunted.
Stalked on street-corners
We slink, they cuff.
Cold steel on bone.
Lock us up.
Take our home
For an open bottle
An afternoon buzz.
They watch us squirm.
They eat our pain.
We are hungry,
Flightless birds.
But
Youthful stupidity looks
Better on white skin.
Light slaps
For the rich.
For us it's
Cold steel on black bone.

That Only Happens in California
Alexa Marie Kelly

That only happens in California
Overcrowded, filthy and dark
Cells for men.
Caged.
Tightly coiled dust
Forgotten when the wind blows
Medicated within an inch of
What could be called "lives"
My backyard is clear
My backyard is clean
Repeat, repeat, repeat
We see shadows of truth
We will know blindness
I do not want to believe
That my neighbors are dying
Trapped dust in ugly cells
Locked in gang wars
Suffocating
That does not happen here
That does happen, hear.
This misery cannot be so close
To home

The Man He Killed
Alexa Marie Kelly

The man he killed will never
Drink instant coffee
Lose at chess
Teach a class
Learn a lesson
Mentor a drug addict
Publish a book
Call home
Argue
Fight
Cry
Piss off prison guards
Appreciate solitude
Feel loved or missed or lonely
Feel tired or torn or dead
(Maybe dead.)
But never indignant and never
Helpless
He will not be a lawyer or
A janitor
He will not be a clerk
Or a hero
He will just be
Dead.

Charon
Alexa Marie Kelly

He protects convicted killers
because he doesn't want them to
die alone.
But
Her life runs parallel
Rarely crossing, never conjoined
to his.
He finds grace and honor
in the men he tries to save,
As his young son watches
Spongebob, alone in the suburbs.
His line of work seeps into
His son's nightmares
Every execution is
a pained scream from his small frame.
He deals in life and death
In wasted time, wasted lives
Too guilty to continue and
too unholy to quit.
This business of execution
Of lost nights, missed snow cones,
Of men dead before we kill them
Of his wife walking the winter beach alone
Of shuttering like Charon
This business of defending the condemned
is killing him.

Animals
Hannah Ehlers

a second chance
without a first one?

born-again?
or born
into another cell?

quick to preach
and quick to punish

hands
where we can see them
hands
on the wall
hands
behind your back
they are not your
hands
anymore

the judge stares back
at you
hollow with a heart
still beating

her eyes glisten with power
they speak:
we are all animals
and some of us
must be contained

Jailhouse Symphony
Hannah Ehlers

This is the jailhouse symphony. The prison yard blues that only soothes the insane. This is clanking metal and shouting voices. This is screaming and the sound of blood rushing, pumping, boiling in your ears. This is hell and Dante is right—there are levels. This is the pounding of fists and the awakening of the torturous voices inside your head. This is your soul floating in the air, bouncing off the walls. It's not yours anymore. This is the beating of a thousand angry hearts attempting to disguise the terror that has become the marrow in their bones. This is a slow death and no one knows if it is deserved. Who would you rather be? The girl who will never hear again, whose heart has gone to the worms, six feet under, or the man who put her there, forced to listen for the rest of his sluggish, empty death, to this? This relentless, animal sound. The jailhouse symphony, the prison yard blues.

Faith
Hannah Ehlers

the justice system
is a multi-faceted jewel
that doesn't shine

it is black and white
in the way
that you are either
black or white
rich or poor
doomed or redeemable

twisted like the rope on the gallows

bloated like old road kill

faith is lost
and you don't expect us
to find it somewhere else?

faith in flying high
every room
is a powder room
every window
is an opportunity
for broken glass
and our bloody knuckles
are our trophies
the bruises that we leave
we hope will last
long on sunken faces
because we know we won't

My Son's Eyes
Hannah Ehlers

oh what I would give
to just once more
see leaves awake in the wind
and daffodils light up
the cracked city sidewalks

to look upon a sky
full of birdsong
instead of barbed wire
and the sun
beat down upon my skin
without beating me down

to breathe in
the crispness of winter
and hear snow
crunch beneath my feet
and the cold fill my body
without filling my soul

to look
one last time
into my son's eyes
seeing innocence and love
instead of hatred for his father

oh what I would give
to escape just one
second of this hell
had I not already
given everything away

Squeeze
Zoé Orfanos

my skin squeezes my bones
—constricting softly—
sealing off the pounding
of my life behind a cage
of knifed ribs;

my head rolls back
—rigid—against the noose
of skin around my neck,
carefully contoured
to be airtight.

underneath the stain
of flesh and sticky
murmur of blood,
bones stand bleached
in silent lines, never white
while I'm alive.

Two Grey Three-Piece Suits
Sandra Majestic

Joey is 7 years old; his father is a hard worker.
Ian is 7 years old; his father is a professor at a prestigious
university.

Joey draws pictures of him and his father sitting at a table
together.
Joey hugs and kisses his father every time he sees him.
Joey says, "goodnight dad" every night before shutting his
eyes

Ian sits in the corner and listens as his parents entertain
their guests.
Ian lays at the end of his parent's bed as he watches his
dad neatly lay out his suit for work.
Ian waves goodbye as he gets on the bus to go to school.

Ian's father tells his son to turn off the TV.
Ian's father tells his son to work hard.
Ian's father wears a three-piece suit to work at a
prestigious university.

Joey's father tells his son that he will be thinking of him all
day.
Joey's father is dressed in a pewter chain-link three-piece
suit by a guard named Mike before seeing his son.
Joey's father is inmate #5673490
Joey's father is serving life without parole.
Joey asks, "What is that dad?"
He answers, "A three piece suit."

A Silent Suffering
G. Gwin

I'm A Rebel due to my views
A different set of rules to abide by
Unrealistic notions—no motion, moving towards nowhere
Considered disobedient because I don't bow down to the
"less pigmented's" supremacy
No leniency for the black and brown.
You frown when we catch a felonious case.
We've crossed enemy lines, invaded a foreign space,
So you created a place, for our kind.
Families broken, dreams stymied just the way you've
intended
In front of the "black robe white face" the deck is stacked
and were dealt a harsh hand of injustice
Outlawing us from society
Stigmatizing a colored youth.
Born to believe that the four yard is our destiny
The things they don't teach us in classrooms we learn in
the cell
Jail, a makeshift university
Professors who have dedicated themselves to a life of
crime and some towards a better way of life.
Injustice is unjustified
Who's going to enforce the law on the unlawful law
enforcement?
There is no justice in the criminal justice system
The time for the penal code violation is lopsided—at least
in our case it is.
The urban youth are prime convictees
All in the name of the district attorneys victory.
A young life sent up-state to deteriorate
We suffer in silence...

Understanding
Emily Blau

Everyone pretends
        to care
        to know
        to understand
But no one knows how it feels
        to be an animal, caged
                a monster, trapped
                a prisoner, broken
                me
Don't tell me to be strong or to hold on or to trust you
Don't offer me false hope or pray for me or keep me in
your thoughts
                No
I know how it feels
I don't have to pretend to understand
All I gotta do is
        sit

        breathe

        wait

Monsters
Emily Blau

two men
walking down main street
wearing dark levi's
drinking coffee, black

average height
average weight
average everything

one man
taking care of his family
working nine to five at the office
visiting his mama every sunday

the other
taking care of himself
working twelve to eight at the shop
kidnapping   raping   killing
his deeds do not show
on the mask he presents to the world

both men appear average
both work and have families
both need coffee in the morning

and both men could be lying on a gurney one day

Money
Arthur Johnson

Money... money... money...
It's what everyone out to get!
Drug dealers, prostitutes, police, people want it,
illegal or legit.
It'll have you doing things you'll regret you did,
Stabbing, robbing, shooting everything above,
But in the end, it's actually showing you no luv.
Think about it!
It's nothing but paper with a dead president
And believe me, dying and going to jail for something
that's nothing but debt is not worth it!
So don't listen to 50 Cent's "Get Rich or Die Trying"!
Because it will have you worshipping it as a GOD
With blind faith and material hope
So don't let it stress you out, drive you crazy,
or go out of your normal ways
Because at the end you're gonna be judged on what you
did to get it here on your earthly days.
Okay, yeah you need it no doubt dat's true
To survive and live comfortable, and to get things
necessary for you
There are people who've accumulated too much of it
Looking down on people belittling them
and that's not right.
Who are you to judge? You're not the all knower.
You're the child of Adam, so you've also taken a bite.
People even occupy Wall Street, just to go on strike
Until the police comes and tell em' to take a hike
Money... money... money...
It's like you've stabbed the entire globe
with a long razor sharp knife
But before you kill em' let everyone know that
You CAN'T take MONEY to the AFTERLIFE

Suicide
Arthur Johnson

Suicide... I'm going insane. I can't control my thinking
I wake up in the middle of the night sweating rivers from
crazy dreaming
It's a problem, a problem dat I cannot take care of at the
moment
But it's been on my mind all day and it won't go away.
I can't control it!
Suicide... It's 1 of many things that comes to your head
Depressed, down, stressed, and sad. You're like, "I'm
better off Dead."
NO! Please don't, it's really not dat bad. Please don't slit
your vein.
STOP! And think about it, about your loved ones, come
on use your brain.
And you're like, no I really have no use here on earth...
I'm hopeless
Just please put down the razor, let's talk...just focus
Have you ever heard the saying coincidence is GOD?
Way to stay anonymous
Well believe it and let the situations play out because it's
up to him
You can't do nothing about it
Because whatever's meant to happen, trust me, it's gonna
happen
So please don't try to be no superman, batman, or no
captain
Just know that with time comes a solution
So if it don't come out the way you expected
Don't go looking for retribution.
Clear your mind, get some air... or take a ride
Because it's really worthless... to commit SUICIDE!
Don't do IT!

Where You At?
D.C.

Simple City, where you been?
Where is the loyalty and love from my so-called "men?"
Lonely, locked down, little me
Why all you all thinking 'bout me?
Nicca, please!
You all aint' thinking 'bout Zek
Stuck, sitting, stressing
A long life lesson
Making money mobsters
I eat jail food, you eat lobster
Heavy heart homie
Stuck, sitting, lost and lonely

Colors
Alisha Carrington

Where do I begin?
Might as well start from the end
Or the beginning with
The now...
Four walls, locked doors
No different from the four walls
And trapped souls from before...
Muggy windows to my heart
Gray and white painted ceilings
Brown spotted floors
Purple faces
Black hearts...
Colors unmatched emotions
Names unmatched to faces
Discolorations of all sorts
Lack of pigmentation
Dull existence
Barely holding onto
The now...
The end is here somehow fading
Into the beginning
Now it's...
Opened doors, free mind
Familiar faces,
But still can't see...
Can't recognize old friends
New enemies are old friends
Once one color waving the same flag
What colors do I represent now?
Pinks and purples
Yellows and greens
Blue skies...
Dark ruby red

Blood pours and seeps through
Stained past
Bloody sheets
Ruined floors
How much blood must seep
Before my heart stops bleeding?
Before I stop seeing these spots of color.
I painted the key orange
The key to freedom is in my mind
And the world is my new door...
A world full of color.

A Tribute to the Life and Work of Victor Hassine
Mikala Rempe

Every moment is a prayer if you think about it
In the name of someone's father
For the sake of someone's son
Always with us in spirit
His life worth living
A life for giving
A life lost
All too soon
A man
A story
The pages bleeding with his sadness
The how's,
The why's
Turned tributes in goodbyes
Chapter after chapter of hope redacted
Without a choice
His life taken
Without a choice
His life given
To us, he is a lesson
Of living without
Of giving for those who will never understand
This sacrificial lamb
He was given nothing but time
And no way to control it
Five minutes to get here from there
Sleep, shower, and slave
When the system tells you you can
Pain exposed in short story prose
and parables and memoir
His life given
His sins forgiven

Amen
I believe

The Power Struggle
Mikala Rempe

The inmate became all too familiar with what the world
looked like just over his shoulder
He felt like he was constantly babysitting himself
Hop-scotching the boundaries of this new world
He could fold his whole life into a knapsack
Like he was one of Peter Pan's lost boys
Needed to make a name for himself
Before somebody made it for him
Needed to align before alienated
Swore to never talk about his family
Wouldn't bring their hallowed names
Into these hollow walls
Learned the prison power struggle
Don't look another man in the eye
Don's bitch about theft
Unless you're willing to answer to a ramshackle blade
You're a fighting man now
You're a strong man now
Man, you're faking it right now
This power struggle is
A lot more trouble than your thought it would be
Never slept so long and felt so drained

And you've got butterfingers
And an audience just over your shoulder
Waiting for you to drop

The Hole
Mikala Rempe

I landed myself in the hole
A hotel where early check out is an amenity not offered
To inmates caught with a shiv for shanking
Where they literally locked the door and threw away the
key
The days running together like the lava in a lamp
The hands melting off the clock
Like Salvador Dali greased the gears himself
Slipping slipping slipping
Slipped away
Slop for lunch
And dinner
Stay awake
Wait for breakfast
Just so you know you made it through the night
It takes 27 steps to walk the perimeter of this hole
I can do this an average of 19 times in a row out of
boredom
Before I start hearing the voices
The whispers
Turned screams
The blur
The blind
The dark
The twisted
Sadistic
The silence like I've never heard before
I smuggled in a pen
Used it like an IV to keep me alive
The ink
Drip Drip Drip
Drop

Wrote stories between the veins on my arms
Traced them like road maps
Fell asleep to the thoughts of driving home
Would welcome the invasion
of the suffocating privacy
If you stare at the ceiling long enough it starts to look like
waves
Concrete and clinical white
I told them I was afraid of drowning in my sleep
It got me out of the hole
Into the rubber room
Beds with straps
And anti-depressant cocktails
Strong enough to kill a man
Or make him wish he was dead
Or worse
Back in the hole
Mikala Rempe is a freshman undergrad studying
literature and creative writing at American University. Her
genre of choice is poetry, especially slam poetry or
spoken word. She has a growing interest in prison reform.

18 to 42
Chavez Myers

See ONE mistake changed my life
In numerous ways
And I'm talking for TWO decades
Not the "Soon to be days."
Who would've thought that THREE seconds
Could mean so many years?
Never imagined my TWO eyes crying
So many tears
With ONE life to live
And a MILLION dreams subdued
The front prison gates
Is where my childhood concludes
Pleaded to TWENTY-FOUR years
And that's just something I gotta do
But, I'll be ready to explore the world
On the year I turn FORTY-TWO

A Peek Into My Thoughts
Chavez Myers

Every since they took me from my family
I will never be the same again
But my smile hides the tears
So you will never see the pain I'm in
Lost in the world, just tryna find my way
Paying no attention to what the people on the sideline say
Cause they just wanna see me fail
Save only a few
I regret coming to jail
But it's enhancing my view
Separating the real from the fakes
The loyal ones from the snakes

The ones who really had love
From those just smiling in my face
Since November 17th I haven't had a real laugh
But I'm feeding off the pain to help perfect my craft
And now I'm sitting at the bottom
Nightmares of the top
Cause when you make it there it's like the hating don't
stop
And I'm scared that I won't be able to withstand the drop
Cause everybody take losses
And the bottom won't be the same
Regardless of how much your loss is
You're still stuck with the pain

Addicts
Rick Lyon

Mark's locked up in Whalley Avenue jail,
facing three to five for fighting with cops--
they'd all wound up at the hospital.
Mike lost his foreman's gig after a twenty-
year run,
              fell off the wagon when his teenaged son
OD'd on heroin.
              I'd always thought Mike smoked a little
heavy
              but his smoker's stink was crack cocaine,
crystal meth,
              whatever the shit is he fucks himself up
with,
              fighting psychic pain with fake nirvana,
              inhaling black soot, spewing toxic mucus
across tables and bedsheets.
              The demon drug scars wooden surfaces,
burns brain cells bald, brings
                              bliss.

              Death, insanity, abstinence--three
choices he'd been given years ago

              coming around again, divorce,
humiliation,
              his elderly parents and young son
powerless to damp the deepening
                              misery,
              the swirling pool that laps at their feet.
              On the wall, a framed photo of dark-
haired young Michael,

   his grandmother's Palm Sunday palm-
frond cross attached,
    whose deep brown eyes, faint smile, never
fade, never move.

Anger
Anne Scherer

STOP! STOP IT!

But no, it does not stop. There is no holding back.

       (laughter)

Louder and louder, escalating with intense emotion. A
jeering cacophony of sounds.

       (laughter)

Overwhelming and incestuous in nature, crawling on
your skin, up your legs and in between them.
"Let me in. Let me in, let me become one with you. You
know I am a part of you."

NO! STOP! STOP IT!

Anger
relentless heaving. The thrust and push heavy and brutal
to the body and soul that longs to flee.

"Where will you run to, you can't run from me."

       (laughter)

"Wherever you turn, I will be there. Look at me.   I
said, LOOK AT ME! You cannot hide."

       (laughter)

The Gargoyle of Anger penetrates humanity. In bedrooms

living rooms

bars

street corners

there is no escape.

And no one hears the screams. They are hushed by hands that clasp the mouth, grab the arm with nails embedding into the skin and with a twist threatening to cause more pain, more harm if that is possible.

Silent screams
Air raid sirens blaze

Auschwitz

Tears stream down...falling on skin streaked with blood.
The stain on a piece of clothing, a wall.
A reminder of all that once was is now ...shell remains.

Emptiness.

Illness
Anne Scherer

       Driven by the insatiable desire to understand that
which is inescapably a cruel mystery and yet so integral to
creation.

       Illness groans, cries, wails and screams its' way
into existence. It scares us...frightens us...the very idea of
being sick or even being around sickness.

       Impaired of our complete faculties to function we
feel incomplete. Rendered helpless we become a victim.
And that is what illness wants...
victims.

The twisted entrails spill forth and wrap around society's
infirmed tugging and strangling life itself.

       Medical care has become highly institutionalized
and people are boxed in, boxed up, boxes upon boxes,
upon boxes with labels like a UPS Store.
Compartmentalized and stigmatized until soon the "care"
for the ill is not care at all but merely
observation...documentation.

Stripped of our identity we are reduced to symptoms
                        diagnoses
                          and mere
metrics.

The gargoyle of illness smothers...
a suffocating embrace.

The fabled "grim reaper" holds you in his arms.
They envelop your body. Ribs break, tendons, muscles
rip and tear. To fight him is futile.

And if you are set free...

You are battered
bruised
        internally
                externally
                        eternally.

Burnt Out
Matt Magarity

The flames shoot up whilst embers glow,
As they imprison a wooden foe.
The logs weep "freedom!" through pops and cracks,
But the fire licks higher in a ruthless attack.

It binds its captives and tightens the ropes,
Devouring flesh and splintering hopes.
The fire is laughing with manic sensation,
The smoke's cheering "end it!" 'midst rising ovation.

The wood's in a panic of mayday inaction,
Bloodied and bruised by the rioting faction.
Blow after blow on the tattered white flags,
Leaves little more than burnt out fuel with little more than
rags.

The victim starts to crumble,
Sobbing tears of ashen shame.
As the fire does nothing but swelter and swell,
Quite monstrously inflamed.

But suddenly the dance is done,
Leaving not even a smolder.
And as we all cry, in smoky suits,
I feel the world grow colder.

Bleeding Heart
Amanda Brenner

Samaritan without her trial
The rebel's sanguine dance
Her cause is something pulmonary
In injustice she finds romance

She stands out among soldier eyes
Red with evils of necessity
War paint too tenderly applied
The most solitary solidarity

She counts her hard-fought sacrifices
The fragments of her misplaced rage
She has to search to find her cause
Her soapbox serves as drama's stage

Volunteer for every burden
Never finding flighty woe
Hers is the bandaged bleeding heart
Stopped short of gush and flow

The Unknown
By Amanda Brenner

Death's the weaker enemy.
Male. Deceased. Eyes: Blue. Age: 3.
Inconclusive Autopsy.

Epilogue
Maggie Brennan

I read now.
Read novels and encyclopedias and short stories.
I read now.
Didn't used to.
But now I got all the free time
in the world.

And I'm starting to think that
my life is all
epilogue.

Bounced into the system at
sixteen.
Tried as an adult, found
guilty as sin.
(They were right but what does it matter?)
Been here ever since.
Wake ups and yard time
cafeteria food and cement cement cement.
My birthday was last month
and I can hardly believe I
finally hit
fifty.

And I'm starting to think that
my life is all
epilogue.

Everything worth living happened before
they sent me to the big house
all the weed
all the girls

all the Christmas gifts
Before I went away. If
I read my life now the first maybe
30 pages
would be from birth to
when the verdict came in.
The end.

The rest would be all
epilogue.
The stuff after the story's
over
and the character's got
nothing
left but the end of his sorry ass
days.

SHORT STORIES

Summer Sun and Strawberry Vodka
Emmy Cairns

I don't know if you ever went on a picnic when you were younger. I did. Sort of. Before I ended up in this apartment complex of felons and guards and cell blocks. My buds and I carried Bud Lite and crackers in an old backpack up to the top of the hill overlooking the city. It wasn't glamorous; it wasn't pretty. The beer wasn't even that good. Actually, the whole thing kind of sucked, but in that we're-friends-and-this-is-what-friends-do kind of way. I guess that's what I miss the most. My pal, Zach, he stayed behind when the rest of us moved on. He came to visit me here once. He always wore this stupid green Nintendo hat. I can't believe he still has it. When I was seventeen, before all this, he and I sat on the rooftop of his building and got shitfaced drinking strawberry vodka and talked about life and girls and how he wanted to study philosophy, but couldn't afford to. I can't help but think he'd have all the time in the world here.

We sat there for what seemed like forever, but that was probably just the effects of too much alcohol and nowhere to be, and we felt the last touches of a summer day. You know, when the sun has just set, but there's still that warmth? It kind of lingers for a few seconds. That's what I miss most. Feeling the sun as it sets.

Now the only picnics I see are the photographs that my ma shows me through the glass every week. Our "glory" days.

Before I became such a fucking screw-up.

If you haven't been on a picnic, you should go. Send me some new photograph.

The Unit
Anne Scherer

Whether you have gone in willingly or have been put on a 24-hour hold, being admitted to a Psychiatric Unit for any length of time is a life changing experience. Once admitted to the Unit the doors to the outside world are locked behind you. The sound of the door to the unit closing behind you is one of hard metal and steel. Much like the doors of a jail or prison. Here too "they" can decide to commit you, send you before a judge for a hearing to decide where and for how long you will be committed or if it will be a stay of commitment where you become a prisoner of the State for a year in your own residence or a group home with weekly check -ins by a local government agency and are mandated to attend a group or report in to a case worker weekly. You have been sentenced to "time" for being depressed. All in the name of mental health wellness and keeping you "safe".

Taken out of your familiar environment and routine you are put on a schedule, your personal property is taken away and put under lock and key. Your body is checked to see if there is evidence of self-harm or drug use. It is impersonal and personal at the same time. The room may have a camera. During the day and night there are "bed checks" where staff opens the door to look in on you. There is no privacy on the Unit. You are clearly under observation and notes are being taken. There are rules and expectations, which the staff enforces. A code of behavior is expected and if not adhered to a protocol is followed ranging from a time out, to the quiet room, to sedation or restraints. When the staff cannot manage a given situation Security is called. They come in uniform and with force to subdue you.

It is frightening and intimidating to see and to experience
and you begin to wonder
"am I really safe here?"

Space to move around in is scarce and there are others
there...strangers. We pace back and forth barely making
eye contact as if this will safeguard our secrets, our pain.
But we are merely fooling ourselves for attendance at
groups is expected and in group, as in Drs. rounds you
have to share your feelings, your pain.
You can try but ultimately you cannot hide on the Unit.

On a modern Psychiatric Unit there are no bars but there
is no escape. The glass is impenetrable. As you gaze
through the windows you can see the outside world but
you are not a part of it. In some cases that only serves to
re-enforce what brought you into the hospital to begin
with; not feeling like you are a part of the world.
Depression to Dissociative Disorders and the full
spectrum of Psychiatric Diagnostic names for intense
emotional pain, which is why you are here now or for
whatever the reason may be. "They" do not always have
the answers.

The question is, do you leave this place a whole person or
one with a broken spirit?

He Walked Down the Hall
Kristen Pulkstenis

He walked down the hall, shined shoes slick-clicking on
the floor and a blank space behind his eyes. The man in
front of him, gripped by his hands, walking to the death
chamber. Strapped in, with pale bands drawn across his
joints. A black shaded window covered one wall, the man
in the chair looking dead ahead. Covered with a leather
sack, like the inhuman figure stalking movie screens. He
left the room. The sound of the chair, two hundred and
forty seconds. And getting rid of the body after that.

The victim, a forty-eight-year-old unmarried male, is the
latest victim in a string of murders attributed to the media-
christened Electro-Killer. Authorities urge middle-aged
black males, what appears to be the perpetrator's main
demographic, to avoid venturing outdoors during hours
of darkness. Reports suggest the killer uses electrocution
as a weapon, possibly restraining, seating, or observing the
victim first. Any unusual individuals or packages should
be reported to the proper authorities.

Journey
Anne Scherer

The heaviness of the dark black sky set in and pressed
down hard on her lungs making it difficult to breathe.
She could not see the stars anymore, only trails of car
lights. Red, white, red, white, they were hypnotizing. She
turned to him, "Please Stop", she said. His eyes
remained pierced and set on the road.

Silence...

She turned away towards the window so very much
wanting fresh air and opened it! He quickly raised it
knowing she would fly. She was his captive.

The forced heated air blew in her faceand she pressed
her face against the now frosted glass leaving a permanent
winged imprint and gazed out at the bleak landscape.

Luther Raintree's Last Race
Susan Nagelsen and Charles Huckelbury

The first time I saw Luther Raintree he was holding a
cottonmouth by the throat. The snake was at least three
feet long and as thick as my leg, and its body was coiled
around Luther's arm all the way to the elbow. And it was
mad as hell, pulling hard backward to free its head from
Luther's grip, the mouth open wide and white like the
cotton that gave it the name. The fangs were hooked
hypodermics, and I swear they dripped poison, although
that might have been my imagination, because I didn't get
within twenty feet of that damned snake until Luther
killed it. Neither did anyone else, not even the walking
boss or the other gunner, and both of us carried
Remington 870 shotguns.

Snakes were nothing new in north Florida summers,
especially in the ditches and canals that paralleled the
highways where the convicts worked with rakes and sling
blades, what they always called yoyos. It wasn't unusual
for a cottonmouth to slither off the bank and swim
through the middle of the work crew in the ditch. The
dumbest would try to lift the snake out of the water or
capture it. Depending on who was running the squad, any
man who killed a cottonmouth, or any other snake, might
be allowed to take the hide back inside the walls after the
walking boss skinned it. Then it would turn into wallets or
hatbands in the hobbycraft shop. Most of the smarter
cons simply moved out of the snake's way as it passed.
The one option that was not available was hauling ass out
of the ditch to get away from it. That was considered an
escape attempt and an excuse for us to open fire.

Part of the lecture before anyone went out to work on one of the road crews the first time included a warning about escapes. If anyone tried to run, the rest of the cons better hit the ground and try to disappear into the clay and sand or risk being shot. I've worked at the prison for a little over eleven years now, and there's never been any doubt that the gunners would shoot anyone or everyone who happened to get in the line of fire between us and the runaway. I was the only woman out there on the road, and I caught a lot of shit about not being able to shoot. One of the rednecks even asked if I carried a pink shotgun. You believe that? But I used to tell the doubters that I'd put a load of double aught in your ass just as quick as the guys. Maybe quicker if you've pissed me off.

The prison had three chain gangs when I first started, each run by one of the Samson brothers: E.B., E.D., or E.G. None of the cons knew what the initials stood for, and they damn sure didn't ask. The Samsons were one of those legendary families that had grown up around the prison and had already sent three generations to work here and had a couple more in the works. They were all big men, heavy boned and red faced, with their uniforms stretched across chest, shoulders, and belly. Never mind the characters in movies, the Samsons didn't wear mirrored sunglasses or twirl a nightstick. They didn't need to; they had us to back them up.

They kept their straw hats tipped low over their eyes, and once back inside the prison and out of the sun's glare, you could see the white crow's feet where they had spent years squinting at sweating and straining convicts. I never saw any of them smile, but then Florida prisons aren't in business to make people smile.

Me? Sure, I wore the hat, too. I'm originally from Michigan, real fair, and I burn too damn easy. Been down here nearly thirty years now and keep swearing I'm gonna move back north sometime but haven't made it yet. My uniform's the same as the guys', brown over brown with a green DOC patch on one shoulder and an American flag on the other. I work out and run, so I've still got a pretty good body, at least for someone my age. I'd catch the cons looking, and I kept waiting for one of them to say something. I guess the shotgun kinda kept them quiet. Well, there was that one idiot from Georgia or somewhere. Lasted half a day, and I still don't know where he was shipped.

At the time I saw Luther and the snake, every Florida prison had two job assignments that went to a special breed of convict with special skills and no problem snitching on anyone. He had to be minimum custody, which meant he could work outside the main prison without cuffs and shackles as long as he was within sight and sound of a staff member. More important, he had to be able to ignore any bullshit about the brotherhood that bound him to all the other cons. In plain English, he had to give a shit about himself and nobody else. The first of these jobs was the dog boy.

A dog boy always lived outside the main prison near the kennel where the tracking dogs were kept. His job was to train the dogs that helped capture escapees, so you can see why the other cons hated them. The job included putting on leather chaps and vest and running through the swamp that surrounded the prison. The dog handler would give the hound the dog boy's scent and then follow him for as long as the training session lasted, usually until the con ran out of gas. It didn't always work out that way.

Once, somewhere down around Zephyrhills, on an August day when the heat and humidity were both around 100–and I swear this is true–the dog collapsed at the end of the training run, so the dog boy had to pick him up, sling him over his shoulders like a damn feather boa, and carry him back to the kennel. Needless to say, dog boys couldn't live anywhere else but outside the walls because they would be dead in less time than it takes for a Popsicle to melt in a microwave if any of the serious cons got their hands on him.

The second job restricted to minimum custody was another southern tradition: the catch boy. Both jobs I'm talking about were classified with "boy" attached to them, with good reason. In southern prisons, every con is a "boy," and the term is meant in the same ugly way that has pissed off African American men for four hundred years. No matter how old they were or what color, everyone with a number stamped on their chest and butt were boys.

If a dog boy was bad, the catch boy was the one who all the other cons wanted to slice and dice. If a convict broke and ran from the assigned squad, the gunners on either end would do their best to shoot him down. The shotguns we carried were all 870s with long barrels, what we call goose guns back in Michigan, because they were designed to reach out and knock down high-flying geese. And all the gunners put in a lot of time at the range. Only rarely did a runner find enough cover to put enough distance between him and the shotguns to get out of range. That's when the catch boy went into action. His job was to run down the escaping con and hold him until we caught up, which naturally took a combination of speed, endurance, and determination, not to mention that ability not to give a shit what anyone else thought about him.

So, in the gun squad's food chain, the catch boy occupied
the lowest spot, only slightly below the dog boy. The
water boy, also minimum custody, was likewise
considered less than dog shit but was usually tolerated
better because he supplied the working cons with water
and food when it was delivered each day, plus he could, if
inclined, do small favors. This usually involved picking up
and delivering packages of drugs or tobacco that had been
dropped along the route where the squad was working.
Some we caught; some we didn't; and some we let get
away just to see where it went. The day I met Luther and
the snake I had been sent from the #2 squad over to #3.
Luther was the #3 squad's catch boy.

He looked like he could run down greyhounds if he
wanted to, around six-one, I guess, and maybe one
seventy, all muscle, sinew, and bone—no spare meat on
him anywhere. If he moved in any direction, and you
could see things shift under his skin. When he peeled off
his shirt, it looked like an illustration in an anatomy book.
But what really stood out were his hands and feet, huge
enough to make him look like a circus freak. I initially
thought his feet were too big for him to run very fast, but
the first time I saw him in action, he ran down a child
molester from Tampa that had a hundred-yard start on
him. He reminded me of pictures I had seen of Jesse
Owens at the 1936 Olympics: nothing moving but his
arms and legs. He had that same natural stride that
looked almost effortless when he ran. And Jesus, could
he run.

We always got briefed on anyone working on the squad,
and Luther had done eight on ten for attempted murder
when he finally made minimum custody and came to #3.
He had carved up some guy in a bar over in Gainesville to

the tune of eighty-six stitches as punishment for putting his hand on the butt of a woman who turned out to be Luther's wife. I personally don't have a problem with that, but I guess that's why I'm a gunner and not a judge. The theory was that with only a couple of years left to do, he wouldn't be tempted to run.

Rumor had it that his name came from his father's Seminole blood and everything else from his mother's African American side, but I never heard it from Luther. And I damn sure didn't want to ask. Those black eyes of his stayed shuttered, closing down any attempt at conversation. Luther didn't say a word to me or a single con while I worked #3. He didn't talk to anyone but the walking boss and always ate his meals alone, mechanically and without obvious pleasure, like it was just a pit stop to take on fuel before getting on with his life.

The cons working on the squad were all close custody, meaning they couldn't move outside the walls without armed supervision or some sort of restraints, and they had usually done something to get assigned to us. The gun squads were generally used as punishment for disciplinary cases, especially in the summer, when temperatures were always in the high nineties and even over a hundred. Funny thing about Florida prisons: if the temperature dropped below thirty-two, no work squads went out, but there was no upper limit. It could be hot enough to scorch the balls off a pool table, and we would still take them out. Let the thermometer drop down close to forty and people started pulling on everything they owned and still complained. As my mother once said when I told her on the phone one February afternoon that the local weather had just predicted the evening's low as a "frigid" fifty-one, "Those Southerners must have frail constitutions."

Given the weather and working conditions, most of the cons on the gun squads naturally didn't want to be there, but we always had five or six volunteers who used any excuse to get outside the walls for a little while, even if it meant pulling cypress stumps out of a swamp or clearing brush in ditches chest-deep with water and fighting off all the local critters, from mosquitoes with three-inch wing spans to snakes and the occasional alligator.

Luther was, of course, an outcast among the convicts, the Benedict Arnold of the chain gang, who had no scruples about snatching another man's freedom. Some of the men on the squad talked loudly enough about him and his mother and the rest of his family for Luther to hear, but he never reacted, even when I asked him if he wanted to handle the situation. Luther just shook his head maybe a fraction of an inch and said, "No, ma'am, Miz Crews." He kept looking over the heads of the men in the ditch like they weren't even there.

I know it wasn't fear that stopped him from getting a piece of the talkers. Fear has an undeniable look, a feel, even a smell you can pick up. Luther had none of the signs, and I swear he would have gone into hell to kill the devil himself if he had a reason. It was like he was immune to any of the motives and emotions that plagued the rest of us out there under that relentless sun. At least, that's what I thought.

When you're working on a chain gang, no matter in what capacity, you count days, not weeks or months, and I had been #3 squad's gunner for forty-six days when a red-headed con named Harvey broke and ran while the crew pulled stumps at the edge of the swamp. Usually a typical chain gang earned its name by putting shackles on the working cons, but Florida didn't feel the need, partially because we were surrounded by swamp with no place to go, and leg irons reduced the cons' ability to get the work done. But primarily because the squad relied so much on the gunners' ability to stifle anyone with rabbit blood in them and shoot down those who were stupid enough to try us.

Harvey was twenty-two years old, in pretty good shape, and told anyone who would listen how much he absolutely hated prison. He was fair, even whiter than I am, so you can imagine how his skin cooked and bubbled under a July sun. He had been on the squad for about two weeks and missed three days of that with sunburn. Hell, he would need an SPF rating of a million to keep the sun from barbequing him. I think he was from Apopka or one of those other little, redneck towns and talked about his girlfriend so much that the other cons told him to shut up. I mean, what twenty-two-year-old kid doesn't? He was locked way with his hormones off the charts and plenty of time to lie in his bunk and think about things he wished he were doing instead of pulling stumps and dodging snakes.

Whether that was what finally pushed him over the edge I never found out, but he had worked himself over to the center of the squad where he was exactly between the two gunners. The rest of the cons had looped a rope around a particularly stubborn stump at the edge of the swamp. Harvey had stayed behind in chest-deep water to push on the stump while the other men pulled. It was the dirtiest job, one that required him to slither down into the muck, place his back against the stump, and then push with his legs. When the cons began to pull, Harvey bent so low that he was out of sight and then made his move. It wasn't a bad plan when you think about it.

I think he probably went under the water for a few yards to get farther into the swamp, because when the we first noticed him, he was already running a zigzag path, ducking and dodging among the trees. As if on cue, everyone dropped to the ground just as both me and the other gunner opened up on him. I knew he had figured the odds to put him at the maximum range of the shotguns before anyone missed him. And the son of a bitch was right.

Popcorn was the other gunner. He had worked at the prison for almost thirty years, most of that as a tower guard, and was so dumb that it probably took him two hours to watch 60 Minutes. At one time, he was another gun squad's walking boss, but his sergeant discovered that he counted his squad in and out the gate by moving dried beans from one pocket to another: one prisoner out, one bean in the pocket. When the squad returned, he reversed the process. If he had any beans left after the last man entered the gate, he had obviously lost someone. To give him credit, that never happened, but he got demoted to gunner after that, and all of us who knew him were convinced that a gunner, not a walking boss, was where his real talent lay.

He was a small man—I'm five-six and we were eye to eye, even with his boots on—but he was eight feet worth of mean. He might have weighed one-fifty with the shotgun, and all of that was wrinkled skin and sinew, including the tattoo on his left forearm that said, "Born to Loose." I don't remember anyone telling him about the spelling, but if they did, Popcorn obviously didn't give a damn. Red Man was his favorite chewing tobacco, and he always kept a cheek full, like a chipmunk getting ready for winter. The really bizarre part, at least for me, was what I

thought was a violation of how you chewed the stuff: I
never saw him spit. The other guards, and a lot of the
cons, chewed the same stuff and spit out the juice
periodically in a brown stream. Not Popcorn; he just
swallowed it, which might explain his preference for
shooting people. I know if I had to swallow that nasty shit,
I'd certainly be in a foul mood all the time.

He quickly fired all five rounds at Harvey, smoothly
working the slide after each shot, one that knocked bark
off a pine tree about six feet above Harvey's head. I was
farther away and got off two shots, but knew I'd never hit
anything at that distance unless it was an accident. Still, I
was supposed to empty my weapon, so I sent the other
three rounds toward Harvey's back. Then I turned back
to keep an eye on the rest of the cons in case Harvey's
move was a diversion or part of a bigger plan. When
Popcorn's shotgun was empty, he lowered the barrel,
looked at E.B., the walking boss and oldest of the three
brothers, and shrugged. E.B. raised one hand to Luther
and pointed toward Harvey's disappearing back about
eighty yards away. "Go," he said.

Luther immediately jumped over a ditch and broke into a
ground-eating run. Popcorn and I reloaded, and he rested
his on his shoulder while he and E.B. watched Luther
close the gap between him and Harvey. The kid could
run, but he never stood a chance against Luther. It was
the '36 Olympics all over again.

Harvey looked back once and saw Luther gaining on him
and tried to run faster, but his legs and arms lost
coordination, waving all over the place, like they didn't
really belong to him. He finally stumbled and fell in a
heap, but the kid was game and got back up. By then
Luther was only forty yards away and running like a well-

oiled machine, nothing moving but arms and legs in a smooth, fluid rhythm. I was still new enough to feel kind of sorry for Harvey. I could only imagine what was going though his head. He had outrun the shotguns but lost his chance for freedom because another con was about to collar him. He wasn't going to reach his girlfriend and a real bed. Instead, he would be spending a lot of time in a strip cell with nothing but a thin, plastic mattress and his underwear.

A little farther out, the swamp opened onto a broad field, so both Luther and Harvey could both shift into overdrive while the rest of us watched the show. Popcorn leaned toward E.B. and nodded. "Yeah, old Luther's gonna git him now. Boy shoulda never tried in the first place."

"You got that right," E.B. said. "That goddamn Luther's a wonder." He pointed toward the two men. "Betcha ten bucks he gets him before that big pine at the corner."

Popcorn snorted. "You shittin' me, E.B.? You think I'm gonna bet against Luther?"

Luther had gained another ten yards on Harvey and was closing fast. E.B. grinned and pointed with his chin. "He's got him now. Watch this. This is my favorite part. Most of 'em just give up and lie down when they see Luther. Let's see how this boy handles it."

"Soon now," Popcorn said. "Yeah, Luther's gonna git him quick."

Like everyone else, I followed the chase and waited for it to be over. Luther took two longer strides and pulled even with Harvey, and we all knew that one of those long arms was about to stretch out and circle his neck.

"Here it goes," Popcorn said. "Luther's got him now."

Suddenly, Luther put on a burst of speed, and I heard Popcorn say, "What the fuck?" just as Luther passed Harvey and sprinted for the tree line less than ten yards away. Popcorn automatically brought up the Remington, but E.B. pushed it down.

"Won't reach him out that far." He took off his hat and scratched his head as Harvey followed Luther into the same trees. "You believe that? Son of a bitch ran down the white kid and ran right goddamn past him. He just kept going."

Popcorn was still looking at the empty field. "Gotta be some kinda game the nigger's playin', E.B. He's probably waitin' inside them woods and sittin' on the kid right now."

E.B. shook his head and pulled the radio off his belt. "I don't think so. He weren't runnin' like he intended to stop. He's probably in Tampa by now, the way he runs. I better call this one in and send for the van to pick up the rest of 'em." He looked at me and motioned toward the road. "Git the rest of the squad lined up, Cathy, so I can git a good count." He looked out over the field one last time and took a deep breath. "Son of a bitch won't get far." He shook his head slowly. "And his ass is mine when we get him back."

Right then, my uniform didn't matter. I hoped Luther would keep running all the way to California and never get caught. I didn't want to think about what E.B. would do to him if he did.

Popcorn took one more look at the empty field. "Don't guess I'll ever understand the black bastards. You do everything in the world for 'em, give 'em a decent job where they don't have to work much, feed 'em better than the other ones, and this is how they pay you back."

E. B. took off his hat and slapped his leg. "Goddamn if I understand it, either. Must be somethin' in their blood makes 'em do shit like that."

Popcorn stroked the barrel of the twelve gauge. "Fuckin' Luther," he said. Then he looked at the water boy and took a couple of steps back. "Get your sorry convict ass up, and don't you goddamn dare laugh, don't even smile. I'm itchin' to shoot a son of a bitch, and it just might be you."

I wasn't sure if he meant it, but the water boy got up very slowly, just to make sure he didn't give Popcorn an excuse and took his place in line with the rest of the cons. Ten minutes later, the van pulled up to take them all back to the prison.

One of the local cops captured Harvey a little before 10:00 that night. Well, he didn't exactly capture him. That requires a little effort. Harvey pretty much staggered out of the swamp with his hands up and surrendered. He was covered with mosquito bites, and the cop who arrested him swore that Harvey thanked him when he cuffed him and put him in the cruiser's back seat.

And Luther? Contrary to what E.B. and Popcorn expected, none of us ever saw Luther again. Sure, reported sightings by everyone with a cell phone and a taste for America's Most Wanted placed him everywhere from Pensacola to Anchorage. Some creative snitch even had him in Italy hanging out with Whitey Bulger. But if it was Luther, he was gone by the time anyone got there to check. A few people said he really was part Seminole and had disappeared into the Everglades and was living with the alligators and panthers and pet pythons that had been turned loose by people who never realized how big a grown snake would get.

Whatever happened to him, Luther's sprint that day inducted him into the convict hall of fame, along with total forgiveness for all the times he had run down other cons, now seen as part of his master plan to get away. Someone even pointed out that when Luther was chasing another con, he always kept himself between the gunners and the runner, maybe trying to shield him to keep him from being shot. It's hard to say at this point, but the cons were still repeating the story a long time after the prison stopped using catch boys.

It didn't matter to the rest of us on the other side; all we knew is that a con had gotten away and outrun two shotguns in the process, and our reputations would never be the same. Popcorn retired a year later, and I transferred over to food service. Whenever E.B. would come to pick up his squad's lunch, we would keep telling each other that it was only a matter of time before Luther got busted. Just goes to show how much we knew about Luther.

That was nearly ten years ago, and I still glance at the local section of the paper every morning just to check if Luther's still out there. He is, and when I refold the paper and put it back on the table, I can't resist a grin when I think about that day when I watched him sprint past Harvey in that last race to freedom and the look on E.B.'s

and Popcorn's faces. They got one thing right that day:
Luther Raintree could damn sure run.

An Overture to the End of the World
Amanda Brenner

Every time the world has ended a man or woman rises to the sky to sing the song of rebirth-a song of purity and beauty that creates a new world from the debris of the old.

The measure ends and the song repeats thousands of times-thousands of chances to learn from our past mistakes. The song repeats. That is, until the scientists and philosophers all came together and discovered the pattern of death and rebirth and fancied themselves kings of the new world. They sought out the girl of the new generation with the song in her heart and lectured and dictated to her open mind: "There is no God, no karma, no soul, no universe, no conscience. We are alone, we are abandoned- morality and ethics be damned. Emotions are fragments of mind- love descended from lust. They fall to waste. It is mathematical, it is a pattern. When the world ends, you will sing and we will rise from the ashes." And the girl nodded and they took her away and secluded her in a white room. The song in her heart spoke of light, but she never saw it. The song spoke of unity, but the world remained eternally foreign to her. For the duration of her lifetime, the girl stayed in the white room-ignorant of all, but uncorrupted by the realm outside. For as the people of the world had learned of the pattern of birth and rebirth, they decided that the answers to What and Why and How no longer held meaning. They realized that there was never much difference between the pious man and the benevolent atheist and so both ceased to be. The clergy and the mothers had rent their garments and jumped into the rivers to be baptized into their unfaith for they had convinced themselves that humans are not

predisposed to be good. And people stole and killed and
hurt, and this was accepted as our natural state. And with
each evil act, the world was darkened with smog and dirt
and black dust that hovered in the air.

They never realized that they were suffocating.

One day when the world was very old and very dirty, the
self-proclaimed kings unlocked the door and set free the
girl with the song in her heart, now a very old woman
close to death herself. Immediately, as if she were a loose
balloon, the woman's body rose into the sky. Her eyes
that had never seen light were quickly blinded by the ever-
approaching sun. With her limbs outstretched as she
hovered and faced the stars and with eyes closed, she
burst forth. And produced...a cough. She coughed and
coughed on the sooty air of the atmosphere and the dust
that she coughed from her lungs fell like black rain on to
the people back on Earth. They pointed to the soot falling
from the sky and called, "Look there is betrayal. There is
deceit. There are all the atrocities we have committed.
There goes hatred, intolerance, lies." And they watched
the grime fall until they were silently drowned in their
own tainted rain, fingers still pointing to the sky above,
transfixed by their own filth. And as the old woman was
overwhelmed by the resulting silence, she realized that
there was no song, no new world. Her race had been
smothered by the dust and dirt of sin. She shed no tears.

She would have smiled grimly at the sadness of it all.
But there was no time. If there was ever such a thing, it
existed no longer.

Everything dissolved.

Mud Flap Girl
Molly McGinnis

Stories on paper always have beginnings, but mine was never this way. It doesn't start with my parents any more than it starts with the cop, or Julio, or the bar across the street from Sadie's Diner. One day you walk in on your own life getting it on with someone else's story. And you take a few steps backward and grab the edge of the refrigerator and wonder how it happened.

I bus tables at Sadie's Diner on 15th and Broadway. Not the Broadway in New York – the Broadway that crosses a spread-out town in the middle of a spread-out state. If this town were a loose tooth, that Broadway would be the string connecting it to the mouth of America. But we serve good pie and coffee, and that's got to count for something.

On Sunday mornings, when I sweep the front steps and mop up whatever guts last night's drunks have spilled on the sidewalk, pigeons fly up out of nowhere. It's like the night stuffs them into the most uncomfortable corners of the building, and my footsteps startle them awake. They remind me of paper planes. They make the manager yell about messes on cement.

I've worked at Sadie's Diner since the summer after high school – just over a year. It's the "after" I never imagined – not the sorority-girl-perfect college years I dreamed up – but not bad. On weekends, in the morning, I'll stand outside and smoke a cigarette and watch the town light up. The sunrise on windshields. The neon blonde in the window kitty corner. A crushed Pepsi can glittering in the elbow of the curb.

Julio comes in at about 9 a.m. He sits at the counter
thumbing through Newsweek or Time, grinding his
molars as he reads. He used to be a ticket taker on a
subway in New Jersey, and when he talks about the
energy crisis or the debates between Clinton and Obama,
his voice picks up that old rhythm, like it's rattling
through a dark tunnel graffitied with insights and bars of
sun. He's got a Super Mario tattoo sleeve on his left arm,
and when he lifts his coffee cup, a smiley-faced star near
his elbow frowns. Sometimes I flinch when he reaches for
the sugar or swats a mosquito with the paper. He asks me
why. I never know what to say. Where would I begin?
With my step-dad, a man on a keyed Rice Rocket with a
thing for Twizzlers and Buddy Holly Beer, and who, even
though my mother was beautiful, couldn't take his eyes
off her daughter?

Julio looks me up and down. I slide him a hunk of peach
cobbler, and he pays before he touches the fork.

"I've never hit anybody," he says.

I tell him I know.

"No one's gonna hurt you," he says.

I smile and go into the kitchen, because I don't believe
that.

When I start the dishes, Angeline's already pumping her
old gospel tapes through the back room. Today it's Sam
Cooke and the Soul Stirrers. An entire choir fits in that
tiny space. It pounds through the Soup of the Day (beef
tomato) and the knife block and the hiss of cheese
sandwiches clamped into the grill. I don't mind. I imagine
the entire antebellum South tipped upside down, or

maybe right-side up, ruffling the watercolor skirts of rich
ladies sitting in tea rooms. On good days, it lifts the grease
in the air.

Angeline leans over the sink for a spoon, her arm hanging
in my face, and steps back, wiping her hands on her
denim apron. Earring-sized triangles of dough are stuck to
the hem. She smells like coconut soap.

"Aislyn," she says, "You been smoking again?"

I shake my head. I dry the pie plate, paying special
attention to the leaf-shaped divots on the rim, scooping
out the water drops like I could find a winning lottery
number underneath.

"I know you old enough," she says, "but just 'cause I'm
old enough to die doesn't mean I'm going outta my way
to do that."

I want to tell her that I didn't go out of my way to do any
of this. You do what you have to. When your step-dad
blows his money at a casino over spring break and your
mom runs off with the guy at the winning slot machine,
you generally don't end up enrolled in college. You find a
job at a diner in town and realize that life could be worse.
My mom writes me letters every couple of months, left-
slanted handwriting in runny ink on hotel stationery. Life
could always be worse.

Angeline opens her mouth again to say something, Sam
Cooke and the Soul Stirrers shuffle toward the refrain,
and through the cutout I see Julio lift a palm to flag down
more coffee. And then a scream hacks everything up.
Outside, two horns blare and someone yells, "Fire!"

Julio inherited The Mud Flap Pub from his late father, who inherited it from his late father, who built the bar from scratch. He moved here about a year ago, after his dad's liver failed. My step-dad used to go there on the nights Mom worked late shifts at the Blinker Gas Station a mile north of where we lived. He took me once when I was ten, just to get French fries, and I felt sure right then that I would never fit into the adult world, this place with thick shutters, glowing bottles propped against mirrors, sequined women propped against men. I sat there and sucked the ketchup off my fingers, drawn to the black light above the sink where the bartender leaned, cradling Vodka and mixers and sliding truck drivers stemmed sculptures of ice and alcohol.

And I had glanced at the woman in the window made of neon tubing, semi-clad in a blue 1940's bikini, reclining on her elbows against the sign that read "Mud Flap Pub." She owned her situation, her blonde hair hot on her shrugged shoulders, like the best thing to do was feign apathy.

And I followed that example when my step-dad went to smoke in the alley with a Latina waitress he'd been complimenting all night, and I let my fingers curl under the seat of the cracked vinyl stool until they touched cold metal. There was something about her that I admired. She was so carelessly sexualized. I watched that silhouette, in her neon nonchalance, and prayed to her like she was the patron saint of ten-year-old girls left in bars. I pretended not to notice the man who took my stepfather's seat, a guy in a heather grey t-shirt with the solid stomach of a mother carrying twins. I knew about children and serial killers. I stared at my reflection in the mirror behind the bottles and tried not to look ripe for dismemberment.

He had a wide, close-lipped smile and his hands moved
about like lead bats, checking pockets for cash, for credit
cards, snapping open a wallet so I could see a collection
of produce coupons, ticket stubs from a Tim McGraw
concert and a membership card for the same national
rifle club my step-dad belonged to. The man could have
been my step-dad, had someone been able to deflate all
his rage.

He almost seemed sophisticated; when he moved he shed
a halo of aftershave and hardwood floors. He was talking
in a wet, weighed-down murmur to the bartender and you
could hear the saliva click in his speech. He had moved
here to be closer to his daughter. She was getting married.
He wanted to walk her down the aisle, and have a Stale
Ale with her husband right here, in this bar. I tried to
picture my step-dad doing the same, and realized, with a
kick of guilt, that I wouldn't want him to.

It's funny, the memories that rise like smoke when you
watch something burn to the ground.

Julio's standing outside in a loose crowd of customers,
doing that thing with his jaw and rubbing his neck with
one hand. Sirens wind cool and predatory through the
afternoon. A fire engine is parked along the red length of
curb outside The Mudflap Pub, and four firefighters in
uniforms made of yellow fabric and reflectors assess the
situation with clipboards and radios, while three others
drive a hose into the smoke and spray down the
surrounding buildings. The neon sign with the neon
woman is almost ignited; she looks like she's being
prodded with pitchforks of flame. She's even more
victorious than usual, smirking, hair coiling over her blue
bikini strap, eyes fixed on someone in the distance. She's

finally free, after years spent under the gaze of oily men
with tan lines where their wedding rings should be.

A Jack Russell terrier trots to the fire hydrant nearest
Julio, and lifts its leg. Julio laughs.

"What happened?" I ask him.

"Beats me," he says, "Guess the ghosts don't want me
here."

I smile, and he turns suddenly to face me. I jump.

"Why do you flinch like that?" he asks, and I notice the
tentacle of a fresh tattoo reaching up his neck from
underneath his button-down. Ever since he started
coming to Sadie's Diner, he's become secretly illustrated,
like a couple of inner-city kids tagged the masterpieces of
the train tracks across his body to remind him where he
came from.

I want to paint Julio an equally vivid explanation, a picture
drawn just as painfully and permanently across my body
by someone else's hands. I would choose a scene from
seventh grade when I sat at the kitchen table after dinner,
bent over English and math books, my shoulders cinched
with hours of studying for finals. My mother would be in
her room, the radio blasting its sorrows louder than hers.
The motorcycle growled into the driveway, the screen
door banged against its frame, my step-dad's drunk
clanging through the house came closer. His shadow
jumped on the wall, swinging a beer bottle like a police
baton. It was the way so many nights began.

Yesterday I saw a mug-shot of a man with teardrops
tattooed on his cheekbones, and the words "Fear God"

on his eyelids in navy blue ink. When you escape from prisons, you leave with scars.

The sirens bring me back like cold water. Julio's scratching his neck, staring at the fire trucks.

I ask him, "Was anyone inside?"

I know the answer – the bar doesn't open for another three hours. Do unnecessary questions qualify as lying?

Julio shakes his head.

"No," he says, "But they better put it out before the fire hits alcohol. If that happens, the whole thing's going down."

Fifteen minutes later I'm back inside Sadie's Diner, soaking up Julio's spilled coffee with Angeline's apron. Apparently someone knocked a vat of tomato beef soup all over the dish towels in the kitchen while I was gone.

As I'm patting dry his latest copy of Newsweek – Global Warming Deniers Well-Funded – our jingle bell bracelet bangs against the glass door and I glance up from behind the counter to see a cop standing awkwardly by the gumball dispenser, like she wandered onto the wrong set. Her graying blonde hair is tucked in a bun, and she has a freckle on her ear like a single earring. She seems vaguely familiar – a distant Aunt? A movie star who only plays a detective?

She approaches the counter, her combat boots slapping the linoleum.

"Ma'am, I'm gonna have to ask you to evacuate this building," she says in a Louisiana accent. I recognize that voice – her identity rushes back to me. I'm surprised she doesn't know me, but then, not so surprised.

She snaps her gum and continues. "The fire over there is getting closer to the main fuel supply, and we want civilians to clear out as a precaution. Thank you, Ma'am." She nods once, and walks back outside.

I join the cop and Julio and Angeline and three women with pink and blue camo-print nails and flippy hair, wearing boxy white t-shirts that read, "Nampa Army Mom's Coalition." I know these ladies from their meetings at Sadie's Diner every Thursday. They order non-fat lattes and rhubarb pie and spoil scenes for each other from their favorite Hispanic soap operas.

The tallest of the three notices me and winks at Julio.

"How's the little girlfriend?" she asks him, grinning.

The little girlfriend. Pin-up girl, mud-flap girl.

"Aislyn's out of my league," he laughs. I imagine myself as he sees me – a too skinny white chick wearing buffalo plaid and jeans with eagle emblems stitched over the butt.

The cop saunters over to us, one thumb hooked on her belt of weapons. Her eyes are bored and hard.

"The good news is, we don't suspect it's arson," she says, "So far it looks like an electrical fire in the back room, which doesn't have smoke detectors. That's a fire code violation. We're still looking into it." She turns to Julio. "I'm sorry sir, but at this point there's not a lot the firemen can do to salvage the building. It should hit the alcohol any minute now, and then it'll burn fast."

Julio nods solemnly, as if to give his history a moment of silence. Still, his eyes glint like pocket change. I can almost see his thoughts racing back over old train tracks, tunneling back into the life where he belongs.

He leans toward me and whispers, "Watch. When it finds the booze, the flames will be invisible."

And Julio's right: I count one Mississippi, two Mississippi, and the roof caves in, and the rest of the structure begins to vanish in waves of sheer, quivering air. The Mud-Flap Pub is being etch-a-sketched back into dirt. I focus on those sheets of nothing.

I notice the cop flicking glances at us as we watch the thing burn. I wonder again if she recognizes me, if she remembers the girl at the motel she was called to all those years ago, on the complaint of domestic disturbances, how the bugs orbited our porch light like tiny planets, humming. I wonder if she is remembering the girl who shied away when she reached to tilt her chin up, examined the scrape on her cheekbone, the five dime-shaped bruises on her forearm. How she shone a penlight in her eyes, and saw nothing. I wonder if she regrets being so young then, and writing it off as a warning, accepting the excuse that I fell in the shower. I wonder if she knows how forgiving children can be. I catch her eye and smile without my teeth.

And I suddenly want her to approach me, boldly, and give me the advice my mother never did. I want her to take my hands and say in a voice that eludes procedure, "It's ok. There's nothing different we could have done.

We live in a world where things catch fire. Let the past burn itself clean."

Of course, this doesn't happen, though I like to imagine it did.

Captive Audience
Karen Lausa

I pull off I-70 at the exit for Limon and turn right, heading south, making a beeline to the McDonald's parking lot, where I gather $1.07 in change for a small coffee. As I wait at the window, I feel sleepy from the hour and a half drive east from Denver, passing little but the familiar exits and the flat brown landscape for miles. It's early April, but there are fewer signs of spring out here than I've seen in the city. A few mounds of crusty snow beside the highway linger despite the intermittent sunshine.

I park in a slanted spot and turn off my engine, tucked in and safe from crazy parking lot traffic and trucks lumbering by. I open my window and breathe in a little fresh air before I head down the road to the prison. It's a good thing to be early, I commend myself silently. Time to sip the coffee, time to feel the breeze and close my eyes to prepare for the next few hours. I meditate with the affirmation of a few birds chirping nearby. Nothing compares to the desolation of heading out to the prison, and my heart is always heavy and my stomach churns. I'm not nearly as brave as it must seem. I'm always a little intimidated, nearly always sad.

Halfway finished with my coffee, my anxiety propels me onward as I head out of the lot and back onto Highway 24, take a left turn at the one traffic light and prepare to turn south on 71, where it's a straight shot to Limon Correctional Facility. I pass the Rusty Spur Saloon and a deserted Family Dollar store, and there's the run-down mobile home enclave where I've never spotted a human before. I always wonder if the correctional officers might live there. If not them, then who else?

There's a short stretch of road left on this journey, a pop over the railroad tracks and then I see, just over the rise in the road, the first chain link and razor wire fencing on the horizon. The last sign of a community is the desolate Tamarack golf course, situated directly across the road from the teal and plum concrete building that houses the main entrance of the prison. The American flag, and the Colorado state flag are madly fluttering in the wind atop the flagpoles outside the front door. It's always windy out here. I grab my driver's license, my reading glasses and a pile of twelve books, and head towards the front door. I imagine the guards up in those towers are looking at me, and I adjust my gait to appear confident and purposeful.

When I enter the main building, the crusty security officer, Carla, greets me nonchalantly. She has a weathered face, and a country accent. She has checked my ID and piles of paperbacks for two years now, and I am certain she thinks I'm a madwoman, driving out to "this place" and running a book discussion group for "them." Carla is a bearer of bad news and rumors: I used to let her gossip deflate my mood, but now I listen and nod and wait for my okay to move outside to the Sally port. Released from the razor tipped chain link cage, I walk towards the next building where I will set up my makeshift classroom in a sunny corner of the visiting room. The Correctional Officer who surveys the activity here is far kinder and personable than Carla, probably because she witnesses the enthusiasm of the twelve men as they lumber in, dog-eared books in their hands, always bearing a big smile when I greet them. During our discussion, this C.O., Kendra, is respectful of our discussion; she checks IDs during count without making a peep. Some officers have been disruptive and halt the discussion to wield their unimpressive power. It's all part of the culture of incarceration, and I learn fast.

We always form a circle with the desks and chairs. Modeling the Native-American tradition, it supports the flow of discussion and offers a sense, ironic in a prison, of equality. As soon as "movement" occurs, the book group participants can travel freely past the green-clad offenders who are polishing every inch of the cafeteria-sized visiting room, as though they were expecting us. In a window-lined corner, I make a one-person receiving line and shake the hands of my book group participants as they take their seats. It is always a joyful moment when we are all there together, ready to embark on a two hour journey into the story we have all been reading over the past two weeks. Me, propped up on pillows in my bed, reading glasses aloft my nose as I cozily devour the pages. My group, in the silence of their cells, turn page after page, learning about different characters who inhabit foreign lives and circumstances that take place in unfamiliar times in history. What threads through the author's words directly into their own hearts, is the emotion, the human responses to life's challenges and the grim mistakes we all make, in the real world, and in the chapters of our novel. Today, we will discuss City of Thieves, by David Benioff. The group holds their books on their desk, tapping fingers and glancing inside their composition book journals with a sense of anticipation, and I am pretty certain that they enjoyed the wonderful writing and charming, heart-breaking story. I pass out a few articles about the Siege of Leningrad, and we glide effortlessly into a discussion. There are always those who received more education on the outside than others, there are those who squeaked through their GED certifications, but somehow discovered the transformative powers of reading in the process. We are all here together to join together as a community of readers. We listen carefully, and do not judge. Questions are a sacred part of the discourse, and they are answered respectfully. The book group senses the concrete walls softening and the sunlight makes its way onto our desktops. I am momentarily distracted as I wonder: who planted those spindly crocuses outside the window? We have two calm, seductive hours to explore the novel, and always, always, eventually, they speak of life in prison. They connect to a wider culture through books, while recalling when "they fell." They are all able to relate to a description of the snap of handcuffs, the bad food they are served, growing children they miss. They describe their own past choices, while we worry about the protagonist in chapter six who is about to make a bad one. There are few ground rules here. I say: "Who wants to start?" There is not much interrupting, few side conversations. Quite a bit of laughter. The book group members are so grateful, I feel ashamed. Ashamed of a punitive system of incarceration that makes my simple, intimate little book group the one program that allows my readers to feel human, every two weeks, for two hours.

I'm the lucky one.

The Execution Program
Harmony Davies

"So I can go home?" I asked.

"That's not what I said Mr. Williams." The woman
replied.

"But you just told me..."

"I told you you're innocent, Mr. Williams, not free."

"But you know I didn't do it. My wife, my kids..."

"As far as they and the rest of the American public are
concerned, you're dead."

"But I'm not."

"But you are. Of course you'll be allowed to move freely
about the island, but you must understand that if it
became known that you are alive our Nations entire
justice system would be in jeopardy. It is of course
unfortunate for you, but you will have everything you
need provided for the rest of your natural life and we
hope to make you as comfortable as possible."

"But I'm innocent."

"I think I have made it apparent, Mr. Williams, that your
guilt or innocence is entirely irrelevant in this case. You
are being more than fairly compensated and I think you
will find that your lifestyle here will prove to be far better
than that which you enjoyed before your conviction."

"But without my family..."

"It is possible that your family could be brought here, but they could never leave. And of course there's the chance that after being told they would choose not to comply, in which case they would be considered a threat and dealt with accordingly. It is your decision, but I think you and I both know the implications here."

I stopped her right there, I couldn't imagine my daughter growing up in a prison, never being able to leave or have a family of her own. "But there's witness protection right? Couldn't you give us new identities? A new home...a different story? We could start over. Something?!"

"I'm afraid not Mr. Williams. While you are not entitled to the details of the case, I am at liberty to tell you, you are not the first executed prisoner to be found innocent. We've had several very close calls in the past and we simply cannot afford to take that risk again. Unfortunately what we've found is that released Execution inmates can't be trusted to maintain the level of secrecy necessary. This is the best option for everyone involved. Of course, if you were unwilling to comply you would be considered a threat and accordingly dealt with."

"I'm already a prisoner."

"I am saying, Mr. Williams, that as a treasonous agent against the state you would receive the punishment originally assigned to your case."

"You would kill me."

"We don't like killing people Mr. Williams, that's why the program was implemented. Cases like yours have shown us that killing an innocent person is, if not likely, at least possible. If it was discovered that you were not executed as the public believes, the entire deterrent value of the program would be compromised. If you prove to be hostile towards the Execution Program and become a threat to its operation your guilt would be unquestionable and the consequence inevitable."

Like the gavel coming down in my first trial I felt the harsh ring of finality in the air. I was an innocent man, held against my will on an island designed to maintain capital punishment in a country whose government could no longer stomach killing, at least not as anything more than a last resort. I wondered if maybe it would have been better if they'd killed me to begin with.

Execution by Association
Tony Malinauskas

Roger shifted in his seat uncomfortably. He wasn't
manacled, at least, which was something; he was also
white, which was something else; unfortunately, he was
also as guilty as the man whose execution he had
witnessed was innocent. And that was something else
entirely.

Aw, come on, his brother had cajoled, trying to
perpetuate a conversation that Roger had tried to end
quickly with a polite refusal, and in hindsight should have
ended quickly with an impolite one. We just need one
guy – this guy's got no family, no nothing. All you gotta do
is watch it happen, and sign the thing to say you saw it
happen. I'll buy you a steak afterwards, I promise. Roger
had balked, and rightly so: he wasn't even a supporter of
the death penalty. What interest did he have in seeing the
state put down some crazy hobo who had stabbed a cop?
None at all, of course.

He'd relented when his brother pulled the civic duty card
on him: Come on, Roger. You skipped out on jury duty,
and now you're gonna let this guy die alone? What kind
of guy does that? You're supposed to represent society.
You're just gonna let down society? His brother's silver
tongue should have landed him somewhere other than
prison guard, the way he wielded it, Roger thought.
And so he'd gone, and listened to the poor bastard
ramble on for a good half-minute about God and justice
and he didn't do it, ya'll are murdering an innocent man
right now, and all that, and watched the poor bastard's
final few breaths, and signed on the dotted line, and
gotten his steak. It wasn't another four weeks until the real

killer came forward, just so broken up that they'd killed the wrong guy, and turned himself in.

And the way the new laws worked out, everyone who had put down the drifter was a murderer themselves. The guards, the warden, the guy who served him his last meal, all culpable in their own little way, and every little bit was good for its own little prison sentence, one after another. Roger was the last to be tried. He had a hope, but not a strong one, that he would be allowed to walk free. After all, he had seen a man die, and done nothing to stop it. The law is fairly clear about what happens to that sort of person.

"Well?" asked the judge, again, impatiently. "Do you have anything to say in your own defense?"

Long, Dark
Tony Malinauskas

A few floors up from the entrance to Hell there is a pipe, a pipe which empties into a sewer so long and dark that the totality of those traits dominate all characterizations of it, and so thereby it is known solely as the Long Dark Sewer, and the pipe the Long Dark Sewer's Pipe. The river of waste and runoff making its laborious way through the Long Dark Sewer, towards some unseen ending, squelches against the walls of the slim, slippery walkways, gradually eroding them, foreshadowing a possible future in which the entire construction collapses on itself and the filthy army of denizens that move within it. And of course the smell is horrible.

The sewer, though, in the opine of said denizens, is preferable to the pipe: not only is the pipe just as foul and awful as the sewer in terms of content, the presentation is even worse, it being the darkest thing any of them has ever seen, extending far, far away from its gaping opening like the throat of a colossal Dementor leading away from its mouth, with which it sucks the souls out of its hapless victims. Nobody knows where this pipe begins; does it flow from a river? Does it flow from a city? Does it flow from another sewer? Does it flow from a thousand sewers, each one of them flowing from a city or a river, and feeding into this one massive, Earth-spanning tube, the lower large intestine of the entire world? Is it the collected product of multiple lowest-common-denominator sewers, the absolute end of the line in terms of disposal? Or is it simply a large, dark, smelly sewer, the likes of which can be found 'neath any civilization in the world, that number in the thousands, the tens of thousands, the hundreds of thousands? The only way to truly find out would be to make the arduous climb up, up the length of the pipe, from its feculent maw and through its twisting, oftentimes-physics-defying, turns, hopefully out to its other mouth, where the waste is collected, and not a man among the workers there could forward himself as willing to take on that task, no matter the magnitude of the greater good it might serve, no matter what light might be shed; for anyone who even made it all the way out would have to come back, and that is something no man in existence would want to do. In fact, it has only been entered from the exit chute one time, and that was to dislodge a clog. This is the story of that clog, and the man who made that climb.

She pressed herself against the wall and inched carefully towards her destination, on her tiptoes, trying to stay away from the river of sludge that flowed in the opposite direction; her nose was wrinkled against the smell, which no one ever seemed to get used to, not even the few rats that dared to venture out into the midst of this mess, which most felt were counter-intuitive, there being not a morsel of edible food in the entirety of the sewer; in fact, most felt that the rats had been put there for the sole purpose of scuttling by the miserable wretches who worked the sewer, brushing naked hands and arms with hairs that housed entire metropolises of fleas, and were crusted over with filth to the point that the rats resembled hellish porcupines more than anything else.

"Who's that?" called out a voice; she looked up and saw that it had come from a man, sitting with his legs dangling precariously over the shit-smeared edge, holding a large rod, with which he occasionally and ineffectually poked at the sludge that was oozing from the nearby mouth. This was the opening of the pipe, the start of the Long Dark Sewer, where the workers took rotating shifts with varying proximity from the dreaded mouth of the pipe; the only two kinds of people who worked the spot closest to the breach were new workers, and workers who had been there long enough not to care which duty they got. She belonged to the former, and he the latter.

"I'm-" she started to respond, but as soon as she opened her mouth, the very air itself seemed to surge towards it, filling her throat with the disgusting, vile aroma and substance of the sewer itself; briefly, before a coughing fit took her, she theorized that the inside of her throat now looked like the pipe itself: dark, slimy, and coated in the kind of dirt that even she, in her green state, knew could never truly be expunged from its place, wherever it chose to dwell. She imagined the taint running down her throat, to be digested in her stomach, where it would be broken down as food was, and distributed by her blood into every cell of her body, with equal discretion; in short, she was now partly filth herself. Given enough time, she expected she would eventually cease to become part filth, and instead be thought of as part human.

Part human, repeated her mind in its own ear, clear as a bell, whilst directing her body to sit across from the man, to take the nearby pole, and to mirror his actions.

"I'm working here," she said eventually, remembering what she had originally opened her mouth for. "I'm new," she added, quite unnecessarily.

The man responded with a darkly-toothy grin. "Are you, girly girl?" he asked, practically cackling the words. He was by all definitions what one would call a wretch: his brown-coated hands clutched his pole in a way reminiscent of claws, his shoulders and back had a distinct slump and curve to them, respectively, and atop them sat a head, the outer of extremities of which were so smeared in filth that his lips, nose, and eyes stood out alone, like a pearl seeded in the belly of an oyster pulled from the middle of an oil spill. His manner, though, was unaffected by this, and his chatting was genial, his laughter genuine, and his spirits those of a regular man, not a simple wretch, who may have been resigned to his fate, but was not owned by it. His voice, too, was pleasant enough: it belied his rearing in any one spot, at one moment sounding Texan, at another Creole, at another something entirely Australian, and so on and so forth. In this way, he endeared himself to her, she who had not enjoyed her time in the Long Dark Sewer thus far, and who was glad to see someone who, potentially, might.

"You coulda fooled me, with that smut-colored jacket and bag!" he continued, this time literally cackling, though not maliciously. Looking down at the aforementioned personal affects, she could see that they were by any measure ruined, that she would be lucky to call them only rags by the end of this shift, as opposed to tatters.

Why a bag at all? She wondered, though of course no answer was forthcoming. Upon arriving, from where she knew not, she had been instructed in the basics of her employ, and had been directed down towards the front end of the sewer by a sallow man; the faces of the other workers she had passed had broken into no smiles or words of greeting, nor had even their necks been elevated or inclined in any sort of nod of acknowledgment – their eyes had remained fixed on the river and on their work, poking and dislodging flow-disrupting clumps of waste, long before she had drawn even with their position, and long after she had inched out of sight – furthermore, with each step, her memory of her time before the Long Dark Sewer had faded, until at not even the halfway point, she was armed only with the knowledge that she was new, that she worked here, and how specifically she ought to move the pole. Why a bag? She may as well have asked why a man, or why a pole, or why a Long Dark Sewer – it just was, as she was, and that was the whole and the completeness of its purpose, as was it the whole and completeness of hers.

"Funny," she commented lightly, poking at a mound of something that could only be kindly described as a compilation of substances more poorly-suited for one another than oil and water, except also with insect feelers (some of them still twitching desperately) poking out of it at haphazard and gruesome angles. "What's your name?" she added hopefully, though that hope was so stymied by the fact that she had forgotten her own name, that it could scarcely be called a hope at all.

"Haven't got one," he replied, predictably. "Although I thought myself a nickname a few days – or maybe it was a month or so – ago. Let's see...nope, haven't got the foggiest clue." She nodded despondently and rested her pole across her knees, her eyes fixed just as firmly on the river as her coworkers' had been. Come to think of it, maybe they had a point: the "waters" were calming, in their own way; they flowed, but not too swiftly or too slowly. Given a bit of faint, soothing, music, she might be able to re-

The edge of his pole knocked hers sharply, jarring her out of her stupor, lest she should drop her tool in; she didn't dare to think what punishment might wait that worker who failed this simplest of tasks. She didn't intend to find out.

"Been staring into the crap going on twenty minutes now," scolded the man, in a cutting tone. "Mind you don't leave something in there, cuz you 'aint gettin' nothin' back."

"What?" she yelped "Twenty minutes? What-"

"There, there," the man interrupted, soothingly. "Don't you lose your head, neither. You'll have no way to get that back, just as so!" Confused, she stared at the man instead.

"Twenty minutes?" she repeated, dumbfounded, "I don't even..." She trailed off, her gaze flicking towards the river, but flicking away just as quickly, in fear.

"Yup," explained the man. "That's the Way it go. More'n a few have fallen in, not seen a one of them on the line since. You're best to keeping your eyes movin', girly girl."

"What is there to do, then?" she wondered aloud, which invited a laughter from him so furious and gale-like that it blew her rapidly-frizzling hair about her face.

"Do?!" he asked, still laughing uproariously. "To do?! Why, you just fetch the checkers, and we'll have ourselves a little game, will we? Listen, girl," he said, lowering his voice and harnessing his jubilation at her naiveté, "it's not a question of doing, it's a question of-"

But she never found out what it was a question of, because at that moment the pipe substituted the pervasive squelching of its ooze for a great, only semi-muffled clanging, and his mouth took on the higher priority of curling into a joyful (and this time quite malicious) sneer.

"What-" she started, and the pipe finished for her: with a scream of panic, or fear, or perhaps simple agony, a figure

flew forth from its mouth and landed into the Long Dark
Sewer, with more of a thud than a splash, and, coughing
and spluttering, began the long and protracted journey
down it that all the other detritus took.

"Oh, my!" she exclaimed, shocked at this; without
hesitating she held out her pole (surely, this was what it
was really for!) for the man in the river to grab onto, so as
to be pulled to safety. However, before the sufferer could
extend a filth-muted hand, her pole was knocked away by
her fellow worker, who then proceeded to beat the mud-
drenched man about the head and neck with his own
pole.

"G'wan now!" he shouted gleefully, enjoying every wet
thwap he inflicted on the even-more-wretchlike wretch in
the river. "Git you movin, naow! G'wan, g'wan, naow!" he
ejaculated proudly, and in that vein he continued, until
the figure in the river had paddled away, with great
difficulty.

"What the...fuck?!" she cried out, horrified and repulsed.
Here, this man had seemed the welcoming sort, and had
very nearly drowned that fellow there! When she voiced
this grievance to her counterpart, though, he only laughed
again, that cackling laugh that she now had come to
detest, and explained himself thusly:

"Girly girl," he lectured her, thwapping more objects
emphatically as he spoke. "Don't you go about fallutin'
'gainst those things you don't fully unnerstand. I saved
that man, shore as I saved you from a-losin' your brain to
that river. That's what are whole jobs is, you see – to
make sure them swimmers don't let themselves get
sucked down, to cauz themselves some clogs – nobody'd
want that, you see?" Having justified his actions to her, he

sat back with the sort of self-satisfaction that comes only from beating a man about the head and neck with a grime-encrusted pole, and then rationalizing it to a startled onlooker. In this case, though, the onlooker was not nearly as satisfied.

"But why not just pull him out, then?" she questioned, gesturing with her own pole just as emphatically. "He could walk all the way down the river and get there just as quickly, all the same! There's no need for-"

"Oh, there's a need, girly girl," he interrupted again, which she was beginning to find almost as insufferable as his cackling. "This here is the Way, and that's the Way we been doin' it since...well...I can't remember since when, but it's been a long time, just as well. So you just listen now," he instructed her, motioning down in the direction she had come, "and you'll hear the Way workin'."

And listen she did, and heard, after a spell, the sounds of cackling, and the shouts of men so enraged and delighted in their fervor that she could practically feel the spittle, the byproduct of their frothing words, spritzing her own face, as they no doubt treated the man in the river the same as her opposite had treated him.

"But...but...why?" was her final protest, and 'twas not a very strong one.

"There is no why, girly girl," he told her, fixing her with a gentle look. "There just is. Now, he'll get down to the end well enough, so long as he keeps awake and keeps a-paddlin'. That's the Way, it is, and it's the Way we do it." And thereupon the bell rang for the end of the shift, and, leaving their poles at their stations, they made their careful way back to the worker's entrance, and from there to their homes, returning the next day from places that they forget existed as soon as they stepped foot into the Long Dark Sewer, as if the air contained in it some amnesia-inducing chemicals, which for all they knew it wholly did.

That day she was partnered with the wretchlike man again. Their shift had cycled back to the closest station, and as they watched the other workers file past, heads bowed, towards the end of the Long Dark Sewer the pipe fed into. The girl was filled with a sudden sense of trepidation, as if a chill wind had just blown past, and she spoke very suddenly.

"What's at the end of the sewer?" she asked, looking down to her left, away from the other workers' destination and down the tunnel, where it got even darker, so dark that the sloshing of the river could not even be seen or heard. She wondered why this was the last station; she wondered what, exactly, was at the true end of the sewer, which is why she asked.

"Couldn't tell you," responded her partner blithely.

"Don't know myself. The last station's a well ways away from it, and the darkness'll take a swimmer long before we can see where he ends up. Walkways end here, too, so..." he trailed off and looked about furtively, before continuing under his breath. "They say, though...sometimes, they say..."

"Yes?" she breathed, leaning precariously over the river in her eagerness to hear him speak; when he did, she had to strain even harder to hear his voice over the squelching and scraping of the sullied stuffs streaming through the sewer.

"They say…they say there's a man down there," he told
her, and broke off, looking about again.

"A man?" she urged him, in a pleading tone.

"A man," he resumed. "By the name of Nance. Mr.
Nance. Mr. P. Nance. Very important man, if I should
guess. Must be so."

"P…Nance?"

"S'right, girly girl, Mr. P. Nance."

"What, like…penance?" she said, nonplussed.

"Don't you go and be 'fallutin' 'gain!" he scolded her, and
refused to speak of it any more. After a certain degree of
time had passed, they could hear the shouting that
signified that a person was making a way down the river,
and he instructed her to treat him in the Way. When the
beleaguered gentleman was drawn into view by the pull of
the river and his own paddling, she brought herself to
gently prod him with the pole, not wanting to physically
harm him as her partner would.

Over the next few shifts, a few more men were seen to
pass through the Long Dark Sewer. The next she treated
much the same, and the one after that she grew a bit
sterner with, urging him along with voice as well. A few
more after that, and she was no different from the man
opposite her; the sound of their excitement would echo
down the sewer to the other workers, who would prepare
themselves for their own shot at the next visitors to Mr.
Nance.

But this truly is a story about a clog, not just one girl's adoption of her new profession, and so you must accept the fact that things continued in this way, with little to no variation, for quite some time, although time in a place such as the Long Dark Sewer is nigh immeasurable; days, weeks, months – perhaps all of these things passed by; all they truly knew was that the bell rang for the shifts, and they entered the sewer and exited it in the same way after each one, remembering nothing about the outside of the sewer while they were inside, and, they assumed, vice versa.

Until one day, the sewer stopped.

"What is it?" asked the girl, probingly. They had developed a relationship as follows: she asked questions, and he answered them. Only occasionally were those questions related to the work they were doing.

"Musta clogged isself," scowled the man. He was a veteran, to be sure, but he had never experienced anything like this, or heard of anyone experiencing anything like this, or, if he had, did not recall the instructions for what measures to take in response. He clanged his pole against the Long Dark Sewer's Pipe (for their shift was the one closest to the pipe, as it was in the beginning of this story) and shouted up into it: "Hey, what's going on in there?"

To the surprise of the two workers below, an actual voice responded: "Uhm...I think...I may be stuck..." It was a quavering, fearful voice, and as insensitive as they were to the swimmers while they were beating them, the two workers' hearts went out to the man in the pipe.

"Well, was bound to happen sooner rather'n later," chuckled the man, setting his pole down on the walkway and standing up. "I'll just go on and a-fech him myself."

The girl seemed genuinely shocked at this proclamation, made so casually. "You want to...go up into the pipe?" she asked, as if had just propositioned her for sex; she was equal parts fascination and revulsion.

"Well, no I don't want, girly girl," he said, rolling up his sleeves and grunting, while the rats that had made a shelter of his mostly stationary body were brusquely dislodged. "But I still am. Got to, don't I? Don't want to get in trouble, specially with-" he looked off down in the other direction, legitimately cautious when speaking the name. "-Mr. Nance," he finished, and without further ado leapt into the darkness of the Long Dark Sewer's Pipe, leaving behind the Long Dark Sewer, in search of the bespoke clog.

"Okay, I'll just..." started the girl, but with no one really to speak to, she 'just'-ed nothing, merely worried about the impending fate of the man whom she now called friend, if not brother.

I hesitate, even, to begin to describe the journey that the climber took up the Long Dark Sewer's Pipe – the mere description of the rankness of the pipe and the method by which he was forced to ascend is enough to turn the stomach of even the most stout, but ascend he did, through its twists and turns, as best he could; sometimes he would be squeezing through a right curve, sometimes a left; sometimes he would be climbing up the pipe, as if climbing a rock face; other times he would be sliding down long drops, his hands scrabbling furiously to prevent him from dropping some unseen distance, to

splat against the congealed mess that lined the pipe, lined
it like the cilia of the colon. Progress, needless to say, was
arduous.

However, it was not hopeless; the air was aiding him: still
it smelled of the worst filth one could possibly think to
have been expelled from the collective orifices of the
entirety of organic creation, but the air was cooler in the
pipe, as opposed to the muggy, heavy air of the Long
Dark Sewer. As the man climbed up the pipe, adapting to
its twists and turns, the eternal fugue with which he lived
his life in the Long Dark Sewer seemed to lift, as he was,
up and away.

Struck with a sudden thought, he called out to the voice,
asking it if it had a name.

"Dave," it responded, after a brief pause of shock.

"What's yours?" When the climber answered, he
answered automatically, without thinking, and to his
surprise, the answer was not, 'I don't know,' it was a full
legal name, albeit one with no honorarium for an
esteemed profession. "Sounds familiar," responded
Dave's voice.

"Oh?" asked the newly-found man. "How so? What did
you do, before your trip down the pipe?"

"I was...a warrior, I think," said Dave, with much
trepidation. "Not a very good one, apparently."

"What was your weapon?" asked the climber, his interest
piqued.

"I...words?" attempted Dave, with enough doubt in his voice to let a murderer off scot-free. "I think I-oh!"

"What, what is it?" called out the climber, but Dave's answer was drowned out by a noise, the sound of metal clanging on metal. Or, perhaps more accurately, the sound of metal falling against metal. David had dropped something. "Oh," breathed the man climbing the pipe, and promptly took action: bracing his feet so that his torso was able to "stand" perfectly straight within the confines of the pipe without touching the sides, he held up his hands palms-flat, over his head, so that they might take the brunt of the force the unknown object was bringing to him.

But by Providence or by Chance, 'twas not a real force, 'twas only a small rectangle of plastic and metal, it's noise having been exponentially augmented by the acoustics of the pipe, and it fell perfectly into the waiting palms as gently as a kitten landing on a pillow. The trouble averted, the man resumed climbing, this time with some difficulty, and at the same time resumed speaking with Dave.

"Are you all right?" Dave asked, concerned.

"I'm fine, Dave," he said, brushing over the entire incident, not trying to embarrass the poor man, who had been through enough already, and had even more waiting for him; in the best-case scenario, he was to be beaten with poles for some indefinite amount of time, while attempting not to drown in liquid feces. "Where are you from, Dave? How did you get in the pipe? How long is it?"

"I...don't know?" was Dave's only response, and to any and all further questions on the origins or properties of

Dave and his trip down the Long Dark Sewer's Pipe, he could offer only a similar response, varying only in negligible degrees.

'Twas not long before Dave had been reached; feeling about in the absolute darkness, the man was able to deposit the object he had caught back into Dave's pocket (as it turns out, it had been a cell phone, but with no memorized numbers between them, and not a bar of service to speak of, the point was moot for the situation), situating himself in such a way that they were now both stuck in the pipe, and no amount of wiggling could dislodge them.

"Well," ejaculated the man who was not Dave. "Shit."

"Do you...hear something?" asked Dave. The other man strained, and confirmed it: that had both heard the sound of...something, definitely. It was a rushing sound. And it was coming their way.

The wave of water didn't come out of the pipe so much as it spurted, pushing before it mightily the collected contents of the wall of the Long Dark Sewer's Pipe, including two shrieking gentlemen, who clutched one another shamelessly as they landed in the now-slightly-cleaner river. Coughing and spluttering, they surfaced, and the weak current began to sweep them away. "Grab this!" shouted the girl to her friend, her brother, offering her recovered pole out for him to seize, in order to restore him to his original position, which she had found distressingly sparse in his absence. The rats were poor company.

But before any action could be taken, her body seized up, as her mind kicked into a gear previously thought to be permanently unavailable due to crud buildup; just as the cool air of the Long Dark Sewer's Pipe had lifted the smog under which her partner had conducted all his mental processes, the water that had washed this section of the Long Dark Sewer had washed away the grime from her brain, if only momentarily.

"I remember..." she murmured, standing absently, as if she was watching lightning bugs flit around in front of her forehead. "I was...I was a judge. I used to be a judge. In a district court."

"And I was a criminal, of the worst sort," spoke her friend, as he made a slow way away from her, Dave still wrapped up protectively in his arms, their heads floating above the muck by the width of a baby's pinky. "And I am off to see Mr. Nance. G'wan, help me along now, girly girl. Help me along."

How I Was Born
Tony Malinauskas

The first time I was born, I recalled the words of the scholar Descartes: "Cogito ergo sum." I think, therefore I am. By that definition, I guess, in fact, I was. But I wasn't much else, to be sure, just a blob of wet paper on my father's hand, breathing from his breath of life, through some unknown oxygen diffusion membrane; I certainly didn't have a mouth. Or a nose. And you can forget about eyes. Existence was short, dark, and when it finally ended, thank God, it was painless.

The second time I was born, I had a face, if you could call it that: a pencil had been pushed into my head blob twice to make eyes, and then dragged through the lower half, from one side to the other, in some perverse gash of a mouth. When the breath of life was breathed into me, I opened my eyes and saw my father, a young, ethnic-looking man, worriedly prodding at my flaccid body. I opened my mouth to scream, to sing the song of the agony of creation, but of course I couldn't. I had no lungs. I had no voice.

The third time I was born, my father was growing weak. It's a tough racket, you know, trying to give birth all by yourself, to something that was never meant to be born. But hey, if he wanted to waste his life to give me mine, I'm fine with that. I had fully-formed and workable limbs this time, if no digits, and ears and a nose. When he spoke, I could hear him, as well as smell the desperation in his breath:

La tecla. Nino, la tecla.

He pushed me through the bars of the cell. Loyally, I went, to fetch the key, but the breath of his life was a finite resource, and I collapsed back into a puddle of sogginess before I could figure out the way.

The fourth time I was born, he gave me the gift of speech: two cork bottle tops, pushed into my chest, and drawn up to my mouth via a length of wire. I opened my mouth to scream, and scream I did. When I had finished, he requested of me what he had before:
La tecla. Por favor, la tecla.
But I can't, I responded, wispily. How can I carry a key that is heavier than I am, with no muscles to hold it?

The fifth time I was born, I had muscles: more soggy paper than ever now made up my body. The breath of life coursed through me, more than I had ever felt before. I filled my lungs with it, a deep breath of resolve, and went.

But la tecla was with a guard, and when I approached, he told me that I must be a phantom, and illusion, that he was dreaming me, and sent me away. My father had given me no brain for to convince the guard to surrender the key.

The sixth time I was born, I had a brain: the same pencil that had made my face, now sacrificed itself to give me the power of reason. It took more life from my father to keep all of me running; he, in turn, was running out. But I would not fail, this time, I promised.

I went to the guard, the one who had the key. Convinced him to relinquish it, in exchange for leaving him alone.

But I could not return with it. I did not have the heart for
to free a murderer, not even the one who had given me
life.

Entonces usted tendrá mi corazón, was his response.
Then you shall have mine.

The last time I was born, it was not the breath, but the fire
of life that fueled me. It was voltage, pure and simple, the
same kind that gave life to Frankenstein, which gave life to
me; and much like Frankenstein, when I turned to the
face of my father, I saw the face of a man betrayed. His
hand clutched me, threatening to crush my lower half.
But by this time, my body was much stronger than his.

My First Hearing
S. Jamel Bellamy

Chapter One

July 16, 2013- 3:35 A.M.

I KNEW I was nervous. I couldn't stop shaking. I even
stayed up all night, unable to sleep; scared to death. I was
in my twenty-fifth year of incarceration. Now it was time
to go to my first Parole Board hearing. Time to find out if
I was eligible for release.

Am I ready? I questioned myself as I stood before my
closed cell gate counting the seconds before it would
open.

Suddenly my hands started sweating. I quickly wiped
them on my state issued green pants, counted to ten, and
wiped them again.

I was scared. No question about it. The Parole Board was
one freckled bunch. No one could predict how they
would decide a person's readiness for release. How do
the Parole Board determine if there is a a reasonable
probability that someone would not live and remain at
liberty without violating the law?

What criteria did the Board use? How did they separate
community-ready individuals from the pack?

Especially since most men and women in prison tried to
at lease make sure they completed all DOCC's
mandatory programs and kept a decent, if not, fairly good
institutional record.

Others, like myself, went far and beyond what was required. Transforming to someone worthy of rejoining and becoming a contributing member of a crime free society wasn't just a concept for us. It became a way of life.

A life different from the one we once lived. A vast majority of men and women came to prison as high-school dropouts, drug addicts, products of the foster care or juvenile systems.

I was no different. I dropped out of school in the eighth grade and took to the streets like I was born to it. Crime, drugs, and finally prison were just a nature progression. It was bound to happen. It was part of my 'rites of passage.'

Older socially conscious prisoners quickly divested me of this foolish belief, and set me on the path to understanding a sense of community. A sense of ownership.

Thus, for twenty-five years I did all I could do to prepare for my eventual release. I earned my G.E.D., attended the anger management program the Department of Correction and Community Supervision (DOCCS) offered, and even graduate from college with an Associate's Degree. Along the way I created a computer literacy program, and a program designed to address the criminal thinking, attitudes, and behaviors of the men in the system. In fact, I had transformed myself from a liability to an asset.

Yet I wasn't sure if any of this would matter.

Not to the Parole Board.

I took part in a crime that left a young man dead. A man no older than my nineteen years of age at the time of my crime.

How do I overcome this foolish choice in my life? How do I make amends to the family that lost a love one? Would my actions of the past twenty-five years even matter to them? And, would the Parole Board even acknowledge that I was no longer the impulsive, quick to anger young man who'd participated in the crime?

These were my thoughts — and fears — when my cell gate finally opened. I stepped out slowly, taking a deep breath.

Was I ready?

As I walked down the steps as all the cells were opened and programs were let out, the men on my housing unit patted my back encouragingly, wishing me luck. We all knew there were no guarantees with the Parole Board. Many men whom never did anything to prepare for their release often received parole while men who actually prepared were denied.

I walked over to the C.O.'s desk and he gave me a pass to the visiting room where the parole board hearing was conducted.

"Good luck," he said with a smile.

I smiled back, took the pass then walked slowly to the Sally-port gate feeling like I was taking the long walk to the electric chair.

As the gate slid open and I stepped inside the Sally-port and waited for the hallway gate to pen, my whole body seemed to shake with nervous energy. Again I wiped my sweaty hands on my pants.

This was it! I thought. I'll either make the Board or get hit with 24-months.

When the hallway gate slid open, I closed my eyes, said a silent prayer, then stepped out into the hallway and began my journey to the visiting room.

Along the way C.O.s, who worked with me on various projects and other inmates that took and completed some of the programs I facilitated, wished me luck.

They all felt if anyone was ready, it was me. But how would the Parole Commissioners feel about me? Would my parole package be enough to give them a clear picture of the 44-year old man before them? Or will they still see me as the nineteen year old angry kid I had been?

Just before I reached the visiting room the Superintendent stopped me in the hallway. "Good luck," he said, squeezing my shoulder. "I put in a good work for you. Hope it helps."

"Thank you, Sir," I responded before stepping inside the waiting area where other men going before the Parole Board were seated.

Of the five men appearing before the Board, two of us were convicted of murder, one for rape, and the last two for armed robbery. Of the five, I was the only one with a college diploma, trained as a computed programmer and had awards, letters of accommodation, and certificates for outstanding community services for the book drives, clothing drives, and food drives my organization conducted. Plus, I had a number of job offerings, and two community centers willing to implement my at-risk youth mentoring program.

The other four had only certificates of completion of the Department's various mandatory programs...

Amongst this group of men, everyone felt if anyone would make it, it would be me.

Chapter Two

July 16, 2013 —9:15 A.M.

FORTY-FIVE MINUTES after arriving in the waiting area our parole hearings began. One by one we were escorted into the visiting room to face the three Parole Commissioners that would either release us back to the community or keep us confined for two more years.

The first person called was my friend Billy. He was locked up for robbing a grocery store with a loaded gun. And, since he was a violent, third time offender, he received a 15-to-life sentence for this crime.

"Wish me luck," he said and then strolled through the steel door with his head help high.

Ten minutes later he was back in the waiting area.

"How did it go?" I asked quickly before the officer let him out.

"Rough," was his one word description of his hearing.

Tommy, a 50 year old white guy was next. He was also in for armed robbery. However, this was his fifth violent crime. So the judge sentenced him to twenty-five years to life. Tommy also had a drug habit which he tried to address...this time around. The other four times when he came upstate with skid bits of two to four years, he didn't try to address his drug habit and continued to get high.

Now he was sober and praying the Parole Commissioners gave him one more chance. His last chance. Because if he came back to prison at his age and with the amount of time the Courts were now giving out to career criminals, he would never seek the streets again.

Tommy's hearing lasted all of seven minutes.

"How did it go?" I asked, trying to stop my shaking.

"Brutal. They kept trying to make me angry."

"Shit," someone mumbled, and I shook my head in agreement.

"Michael Richards," the C.O. called and held the door open.

Michael stood slowly. Like me, he had served twenty-five years for killing someone. But, unlike me, he didn't program; he didn't involve himself in any positive activities. Instead, he fought, sold drugs, and got high. To make matters worse, he just got out of the Special Housing Unit— commonly known as the box — six months ago. And now he was appearing before the Parole Board asking them to let him go.

When I asked him about programming or getting involved with the positive activities, he said, "Why bother? The Parole Board ain't lettin' me go anyway,"

"Good luck," I said.

Michael gave me a long, hard stare. "Luck ain't got nothin' to do with it, Jeff. It's game time, and I'm up to bat."

I watched him walk through the door leading into the visiting room and shook my head. He was 49 years old and still had a kid's mentality. Learning pro-social skills just wasn't his thing.

The best thing Michael had done for himself was earning his G.E.D. while in the Box. So I guessed he wasn't stupid. He read business books. History books. Psychology books. Yet failed to internalize any of the information.

Michael came out eleven minutes later with a smile on his face.

"How was it?" I asked.

The smile quickly left his face. "Nerve wrecking. They act like he have to kiss their ass to get released. Fu..." he paused, glanced at the C.O. then left the waiting area.

"John Franklin," the C.O. called.

John stood up. He paused as if waiting for me to say good luck. But I didn't. John was serving time for raping several young girls between the ages of nine and fifteen. If this

had been his first time in prison for rape, I might have
wished him good luck. But no, this was John's third time,
and I had no sympathy for him. As far as I was
concerned, he could rot in prison.

John spent fifteen minutes with the Parole
Commissioners. When he came out I could tell he was
mad as hell.

"Them bastard kept harping on my crime. I don't think
they even looked at my parole package," he complained
as he left the waiting area.

Now it was my turn. I was the last one left...

Chapter Three

July 16, 2013 —10:02 A.M.

"JEFFREY GIBBS," the C.O. called.

I stood up slowly, adjusted my green state issued shirt,
fixed my glasses properly on my nose, patted my graying
hair, and inhaled deeply. It was now or never, I told
myself as I entered the visiting room and stopped just
inside the doorway.

On any other day tables and chairs were situated around
the visiting room for offenders and their visiting family
members. Today, all the chairs and tables had been
placed along the back wall. Even the C.O's desk that
normally sat up front on a platform had been moved. In
front of the platform sat one long table, behind which, in
cushioned chairs, sat three Parole Commissioners: one
woman and two men.

They stared at me as i made my way toward the single hardback chair acing the table. Off to my right, in another cushioned chair, sat the former Senior Correctional Counselor now called Senior Offender Rehabilitation Coordinator, Ms. Mitchell.

She gave me an encouraging smile while, to my way of thinking, told me I would be all right.

I say down and faced the three Parole Commissioners: Ms. Sanchez, Mr. Ronald, and Mr. Jackson. These three would determine my readiness for release.

I inhaled deeply.

"My name is Commissioner Jackson, and this is Commissioner Sanchez, and Commissioner Ronald. We are here to decide if, at this time, you are ready to live at liberty without again violating the law. Please state your name and number for the record."

Although I taught public speaking classes, and gave lectures during Black History Mont, Spanish Heritage Month, and other functions throughout the year, my tongue suddenly stuck to the roof of my mouth. Every time I tried to speak, I'd stutter as if I had a speech impediment. "Umm," I choked.

Commissioner Sanchez laid down the folder she was reading and stared across at me with dark eyes covered by gold framed glasses. "Take your time. We are here for you. So don't worry, we're not going anywhere."

"Thank you," I said, trying to smile even though I heard the sarcasm dripping from her carefully phrased words.

And, for some reason, hearing her condescending tone
seemed to settle me. The Commissioners were not there
to be my friend. They had come to judge me and
determine my readiness for release. Nothing more and
nothing less.

With this thought planted firmly in my head, I became
calmer, more relaxed.

"My name is Jeffrey Gibbs, 89B0001," I said confidently.

For the next fifteen minutes my confidence was
reinforced by the questions and tone of the interview.

While Commissioner Sanchez read through the parole
package I submitted with all my plans and
accomplishments, Commissioner Jackson said, "Tell us
about the crime."

As I tried to explain the events leading up to that ill fated
day, I fidgeted in my seat, praying the Commissioners
didn't misread my fidgeting as untruthfulness. But
discussion the chain of events that lead up to a young man
dying seemed, in hindsight, so stupid.

"Well, Sir, it all began when we got into a fight with Mr.
Billups and his friends at the neighborhood pool after I
spoke to his girlfriend. From that moment on we became
sworn enemies. Any time one of our groups say someone
from the other group we fought. Then one of my friends
was shot and killed. And like the kids that we were, we
believed that we had to respond in kind. So it was
suggested that we shoot up their hang out spot. So, um,
we got together that night, rode our dirk bikes over to
their hang out spot and opened fire. We didn't find out
until the next day that we had killed someone," I said

slowly not realizing that tears were running down my cheek at the senselessness of taking a human life.

"We see that you wrote a letter of apology to the family. We also see that you worked with the local district attorney to develop an at-risk mentoring program..."

Upon hearing this I smiled and wiped my eyes. The mentoring program was one of my signature accomplishments.

"We also note that you completed Aggression Replacement Training and served as its IPA facilitator for three years. You earned a college degree, taught computer literacy, public speaking, Manhood Responsibility, and other programs. You have an impressive record. Your last misbehavior report was in 1991, a Tier II for disobeying a direct order," Commissioner Jackson said, staring across at me. "Very impressive record."

I fought to hide my smile. "Thank you," I said with as much modesty as I could muster.

"Does anyone else have any more questions?" he then asked.

"No," Commissioner Sanchez answered.

"Just one," Commissioner Roland sad. "We read your parole package, but I would like to hear this from you. What are your plans for release?"

"Sir, I have received several job offerings to work as a peer counselor for at-risk youth with a beginning salary of $45,000.00 a year. Further, along with my wife of ten years, who I will be living with upon release, we have begun the process of starting our own foundation whose mission is to provide scholarships to at-risk youths who just need support in order to fulfill their potential. There are two letters inside of my parole package from two prestigious foundations that signed on to provide the initial grant money for this endeavor. Also, as part of my civiv duty, I will volunteer my time and energy to speak to juveniles on Riker's Island, and those in group homes and in foster care."

"Do you have another question?" Commissioner Jackson asked, giving me the impression that he would vote to release me.

"No, that's all for now," Commissioner Roland said.

"Do you have anything else you would like to add?" Commissioner Jackson said, turning to me.

I inhaled deeply. Most offenders, when asked this question, usually answer, No. But this was the time to make sure everything you needed to say, was said. At least that's what I've been told.

So I took a deep breath and gave them my heart filled unprepared presentation.

"Yes, Sir, I do. I would like this Board to know that if I could go back in time and change anything about my life, it would be that ill conceived day to go along and participate in a crime that left a young man dead. My crime not only devastated his family, but deprived the community of a future leader, doctor, or teacher," I said, letting my tears show my remorse. "Since coming to understand the catastrophic aftermath of my crime, and

the pain and suffering it has caused the victim's family, I
made it my life's mission to make sure Roberts's name
would live on, if only vicariously, by naming the
scholarship the Robert Billups scholarship for outstanding
community and educational services. The scholarship was
named with Mr. Billups' mother and sisters permission."

"Do you have anything else you would like to add?"
Commissioner Jackson asked again.

"No, Sir."

"You will receive our decision in the mail within seventy-
two hours."

"Thank you, Ma'am and Sirs," I said, coming to my feet
and damping the impulse to go shake their hands.

Ms. Mitchell walked me to the door and whispered, "You
did good."

I smiled and said, "Thank you," as I left the visiting room.
I did all I could do to make myself community ready.
Now it was up to the Parole Commissioners...

Chapter Four

July 18, 2013 —4:30 P.M.

WHEN LEGAL MAIL was called and my cell gate
opened, I nearly fainted. Today was the day I would learn
my fate.

I dressed quickly, walked downstairs and waited for the
officer in the control bubble to open the Sally-port gate.

Since he was a regular for old timer as we prisoners called
them, he opened both fates" the one leading into the
Sally-port and the one opening to the hallway.

I silently thank him for not making me wait for one gate
to close before the other one opened. I stepped out and
quickly walked to the small office where legal mail was
given out. Along the way I ran into Billy and Michael.
"What's good?" I asked just to have something to say.

"We'll know in a minute," Michael answered, and Billy
and I smiled.

For the last two days word had spread around prison that
out of the five people who went before the Parole Board,
only one made it. Everyone believed that one was me.
After all, I was the most prepared for release. I had
accepted responsibility for my crime, sought ways to
change my criminal attitudes and behaviors, and even
reached out to the victim's family. His mother and sisters
wrote letters of support for my release. If the could
forgive me what reason would the Board have to keep me
in prison.

As Billy, Michael and I reached the small office, John
Franklin and Tommy Hines were coming out.

"What it say?" Billy quickly asked.

Tommy showed us his thick envelops for an answer. We
sighed. It was common knowledge that when a person
received a thick envelope, that person had been denied
parole. Inside of the envelope was the board's decision
and the appeal papers to challenge their decision.

"Damn, man," I said.

John Franklin flashed his thick envelope and quickly walked off. He knew we didn't like him, and we made no secret about it.

"After you," Michael said, holding the door open for Billy and me to enter the office.

"No, after you," Billy said, giving away his anxiety, his fear of what awaited us.

"Move out of the way," I said to them both and entered the office, immediately walking to the C.O.'s desk in the center of the room.

"Name and number," the officer said.

After giving him my name and number, he cut open the thick envelope and handed me the Parole Board's decision which I proceeded to read out load. "After careful consideration and noting your many accomplishments and institutional record, we find that at this time, there is a reasonable probability that you would not live and remain at liberty without violating the law."

I glanced at Michael and Billy. "Can you believe this bullshit! They even hit me for the serious nature of the crime. The judge gave me twenty-five years for the nature of the crime," I said, stuffing the decision back in the envelope. My next Board appearance was scheduled for July 2015.

I left the office shaking my heard. If their decision to keep me in prison for two more years wasn't bordering on irrational, arbitrary and capricious, nothing was.
The thing I couldn't understand was: what more could I have done to prove my readiness for release. I had a job and place of residence waiting for me. I had support from the district attorney, the judge, and more importantly the victim's family. Still the Board denied me parole. The sad reality is that I wasn't the only community ready individual the Board had done this to. The prison system was filled with men and women whose criminal days were over, who would never commit another crime again. So why keep them in prison? Why waste taxpayers' dollars? If public safety was the issue, statistics clearly showed that those least likely to re-offend were people convicted of murder and those with college degrees.

And that's why I couldn't understand any of it. So i moped around the housing unit for the rest of the day, making calls and letting my family know I wouldn't be home this year. "Maybe in 2015, if the Court doesn't overturn the Board's decision," I said, hoping this would cheer my wife up, yet knowing she was dying inside.

When the men returned from evening recreations, I learned that the person who made the board was none other than Michael Richards, the one person no one even thought had a chance.

In the coming weeks, other men would adopt Michaels' position that programming and addressing one's criminal's attitudes and behaviors didn't matter. If Michael could make the Board after spending most of his time in the Box, anyone could do it. Programming and participating in the positive activities were now believed to

be for fools and weak-minded individuals. "I'ma do me,"
one bright and bushy-eyed young man said.

I could only shake my head. The Board said they worried
about undermining respect for positive transformation.
One couldn't exist without the other. When they did, the
public paid the price in the form of crime.

After lock-in time, I laid down and began preparing for
my 2015 release. The Board's decision would not change
the person I had become If anything, it only made me
more determined. Plus, it gave me two more years to
continue helping other men become community ready.

The End.

Walla Walla
Arthur Longworth #299180, C-238

Corey lay on his bunk, the newspaper he had swiped form the guard station help up in front of him. "Danny's on his way back," he announced.

"McNeil?" Jonny asked, climbing onto his own bunk to give Little Matt enough space to wash laundry in the back of their cramped cell.

"Yeah."

"Jesus! He was only out a month." Matt's arms were submerged to the elbow in the soapy water of the laundry bucket.

"Twenty-six days," Jonny corrected, working the math out in his head. The news surprised him. Jonny knew an endless line of prisoners who had been released and returned, but he had not thought Danny would be one. Danny had left determined to make it, to not come back. He and Jonny had talked many times about his plan to go to Alaska and get on a fishing crew, to work hard on a fishing boat until he had enough money to return to Seattle and start his own business. He had wanted a tattoo shop. That was his goal in life. His dream.

Danny's idea to fish in Alaska came from an article he read in a National Geographic. Jonny knew that it was probably not a good idea to plan a future based solely on something you read in a magazine. But what alternative did they have in here? Inside these walls, people learn how to live in prison, not out of it.

"They popped him on a couple Robbery 1's," Corey said, still reading the article.

"He'll get all day for that," Matt said, pouring the discolored water form the laundry bucket into the toilet.

Jonny knew he was right. Danny was twenty-seven, the same age as him and Matt, and a guy coming in at that age with armed robberies would be parked, maybe even struck-out.

Jonny remembered when Danny first came to the joint at nineteen for vehicular assault. He had hit someone in a crosswalk after drinking at a party. He had not seemed to Jonny like the type to get sent to prison. But his beef, as opposed to any form of street crime, defined assignments to a specific type of person. Anyone could get drunk and decide that driving was a good idea; fewer people found themselves inclined toward armed robbery. But it was the leap from one to the other that gave Jonny pause. How did a person go from hitting someone while driving drunk to armed robbery.

Jonny knew the answer. How could he not? It was all around him—the womb inside which they were warehoused, then spit back into a society they no longer knew, that no longer recognized them. The reproductive chamber of a malignant stone-faced bitch who, despite how much her children avowed their hatred for her, nurtured them in a way that compelled them to return.

"I can't believe guys get out and come back," Matt said, echoing words Jonny had uttered many times himself.

"Who in their right mind would come back to this? Just
give me a chance..."

"It's not as easy as you think," Corey said, lowering the
newspaper. "Motherfuckers think that when they get out,
they've made it. That's all there is to it. They think getting
out is moving on to the promised land they've dreamed
about all the years they were in this shit hole, the dream
they've used to hold themselves togethers in here. The
problem is, it's not that easy. You get out and find out you
don't know shit. Nothing is like you thought it would be,
like you lied to yourself for years telling yourself it would
be. People are running around everywhere out there and
they know exactly what they're doing. And you don't
know a goddamn thing." Corey sat up on the bunk.
"Think about it. All of a sudden you're out there in a
world where everything costs money and you don't have
nothing but the forty bucks they kicked you out with. Not
even that, because they make you buy your bust ticket
with it. Where are you going to stay? Even if you had
money, it wouldn't do you no good because you don't
know how to do nothing. Where are you going to work?
When you fill out a job application, what are you going to
put down for work history? You going to tell them that up
until that point you've spent your whole life in the joint?
Ain't no one going to hire your. And, believe me, that's
just the start of your problems. out there."

Jonny remained quiet. Corey was speaking from
experience, so Jonny was unable to respond and knew
Matt couldn't either. Neither of them had ever been
released from prison, nor lived a day of their adult lives
on the other side of its walls.

"I'll tell you something else, "Corey continued, looking
directly at Jonny. "Some motherfuckers get released from

IMU. Can you imagine that? Going straight from a long-term isolation cell to the streets?"

Jonny could not imagine it. He tried, but nothing was there. All he could relate to was his own experience of being dumped back out into the prison's general population after his two year stay in that place, which had been almost more than he could handle. Being thrown into the free-world from there was inconceivable.

"Those are the guys who end up coming back for the hideous shit," Corey said. "Like Tank. Or Louie. Or Gangster. Think of one motherfucker that isn't true for. You can't. It's like prison broke something in them, fucked them up. Why would you do that to people—fuck them up then release them into a world that operates under entirely different rules, a world full of people who have no idea what's being unleashed on them? The motherfuckers who run prison are either really stupid, or they want it to be exactly what it is, an industry that perpetuates itself."

"Brady was in IMU when they let him out," Matt said thoughtfully, speaking about his older brother, the one who caught the murder beef three months after his release. "He did his last year and a half there."

Corey raised his eyebrows and again looked at Jonny.

A Christmas Party
An excerpt from the book:
FACES An Unexpected Journey with Unexpected
Friends
Betty May

The holiday season in a prison is as hectic as anywhere
else. Red and green decorations cover the walls and hang
from the ceiling and paper menorahs adorn the bulletin
boards. There are parties in the cellblocks and small
gatherings of the various volunteer groups. Christmas
music blares from the cells and offices just as it does in
the outside world. The inmates look forward to a special
dinner—second only to the Thanksgiving spread.
The biggest celebration is the Family Christmas party. I
was asked to don my clown persona and entertain. It
sounded like fun and I looked forward to meeting the
women's families.

On the day of the party getting into the prison with my
equipment was not easy. Usually, when I attend meetings
with the women, I only have the basics: notebook,
pencils, pens, and perhaps a book or two. For the party I
was loaded down with a large red duffel bag stuffed with
magic tricks and juggling paraphernalia, a satchel full of
balloons, a balloon pump, a ukulele, and a sheaf of
music. Everything had to be x-rayed, searched, and
inspected. The gatehouse was crowded with partygoers,
but they were patient as the officers went through my
clown gear.

The only beings that had difficulty with my presence were the drug-sniffing dogs. They were completely put off by the smell of greasepaint and jutted their muzzles in and around my face and wig with "What-the-hell-is-that-stuff?" looks in their eyes. A bit of pre-entertainment for the handlers, the officers, and the attendees.

A little boy, frightened by the crowd, the noise, and the uniformed officers, hid behind a trash receptacle and refused to go through the gigantic metal detector. I whipped out a long yellow balloon, blew it up, and twisted it into a flower.

I knelt and handed it to him. "Give this to your Mommy," I whispered. "It will make her happy."

He seized the flower with both hands and trotted through the machine, proud to have a gift for his mom.
The party took place in the prison gym—usually a grey/green venue devoid of any joy. Now it was transformed. Homemade red and green chain links looped around the room, and crafted poinsettias and holly sprigs bloomed in every corner. Hand printed signs lined the walls: Merry Christmas, Happy New Year, and a few wishing everyone a Happy Hanukkah.

It was pretty much like any other Christmas get-together. There were 200-300 people present. The kitchen staff provided a beautiful buffet lunch and a group of young women presented a Christmas play and led the crowd in a medley of carols. And, of course, Santa made a visit with donated presents. I did a little show and made balloon animals for all the kids. It was fun and everyone had a good time.

Until it was time to leave.

About fifteen minutes before the scheduled closing, I spotted a little girl, three or four years old, sitting on an older girl's lap, sobbing. I approached her.
"Can I help?" I asked. "Did she hurt herself?"

"No," the older girl replied as she rocked her little sister.

"I told her the party will be over soon and she doesn't want to leave Mommy."

I felt tears, but choked them back. Clowns don't cry. I felt so helpless. I made her a balloon dog. I even made a leash for the dog. It didn't help.

When the time came for the visitors to leave, the officers lined them at the gym door. They would be taken into a small room where they would wait until count had cleared and all the inmates had been checked for contraband—a humiliating experience that involves inspection of every body orifice. The women were separated and sent to the bleachers, where they sat and cried and waved to their loved ones.

The guests were on their way out when a little boy shouted, "Mommy! Mommy!" He broke from the crowd and ran to his mother. He threw his arms around her neck and wouldn't let go. An officer had to pry him out of his mother's arms. The strained look on the officer's face told me she was as upset about the heartbreaking tears as everyone else. She carried the child to a woman I assumed to be the boy's grandmother. She clutched him to her and patted his back. The crowd filed out, the little boy's sobs still echoing in the gym.

I heard a child's voice. "Why is the clown crying?"

Chigger
William F. Roth

On his way to the beach Chigger stopped at a fast food
place. Since yesterday morning he had eaten nothing. He
was beginning to feel dizzy and that was bad; he did not
want to get dizzy. He bought a cheeseburger and a
chocolate milkshake, which left only seventeen cents.
Holding the coins in his hand -- a dime, a nickel, two
pennies -- Chigger wondered what he could buy with
seventeen cents? Nothing much, nothing that he could
think of. Finding an empty table he carefully lay the coins
in a line, turning them all face up, wondering vaguely how
long it would take for some kid to scoop them into his
pocket, some kid who would probably see them as a
treasure? When Chigger was younger, whenever he found
money, usually a coin lying on a sidewalk or floor, he
would not run off and try to spent it immediately but
would keep it in his pocket; he would hold it in his hand
in his pocket feeling that it was very special.

Well, now he was creating something special for some
other kid with his last seventeen cents. That was good.
The over-weight teenager dropped an old movie ticket
stub from his pocket onto the table as well, then decided
to eat outside where he could be alone. Pushing through
the glass door, out of the coolness, he slammed into the
burning wall of humid air. Shrieking gulls gathered in the
air above as he put his tray down on a table, streamline
white scavengers diving and bickering indignantly. Chigger
counted six of them strutting about on the red tiles,
fighting over a piece of hotdog bun somebody had
dropped, pecking at each other as well as the bun in their

greed -- peck, peck, peck. Chigger thought, "No dignity, seagulls; I should kill them."
Sliding his hand into his raincoat pocket the young man felt the steel of the revolver. If he killed these, however, if he shot these gulls, more would land, probably start eating the carcasses, fighting over the bloody carcasses as well as the hotdog bun. Killing these gulls would not make any difference; it would not matter. He shook his head dejectedly. Nothing really made a difference; nothing really mattered any more, nothing at all.

Chigger did not sit at the table but remained standing as he nervously ate half of the cheeseburger, took a quick sip from the shake. Then, suddenly, he put everything down and walked away toward the car leaving his trash on the table, not throwing it into the bin the way his mother had taught him to. And how ridiculous was that? Turning back, he reached to pick the trash up but, instead, tipped the milkshake cup over so that the brown liquid spilled across the table and dripped onto the tiles...And so what? He kicked angrily at a gull causing a flurry of flapping wings and a shrill protest. His mother would be mad at him. But so what?

Driving toward the beach Chigger realized he was almost out of gas. No gas, no money. He parked his car in a no-parking zone, left the keys in the ignition, rolled the windows up and locked the doors. And how many days, how many tickets would it take, he wondered, for the police to figure out his vehicle was there to stay? Moving though the dunes, the pale young man wandered halfway down to the waters edge, stood staring at the ocean, at the small waves breaking so cleanly over the sand. His pockets were empty now except for the revolver he had stolen; they were totally empty. Searching carefully through all of them with probing fingers he felt nothing, not even a shred of tissue buried in the threads of a lining. That made him sad. He wanted so very much to find something, to feel something. But he could felt nothing, nothing in his pockets, nothing in his life. All he felt was the numbness that lay not only in him, but all around him as well. The people who had been floating by for these last several weeks, these last several months, these last several years no matter how they might pretend, were just as numb. They were all just faking it. He nodded to himself. They were all just faking it; he had sensed nothing real in them either. Eventually, Chigger had decided that if he could get just one person to actually feel something, to feel something real, just one other person, maybe it would help him, maybe he could feed off what that person was experiencing, maybe he could come alive for just one more instant, feel something just one more time.

And that would be enough.

As he stood staring at the sea Chigger heard noise behind. A mother struggled out onto the beach with her seven or eight year old son trailing behind. The little boy, a towel around his neck, two blue folding chairs and an inner-tube in his arms, was fat. The mother, who carried a cooler and a beach umbrella, wore a floppy-rimmed yellow straw hat with red and blue cloth flowers around the front edge that jiggled as she trudged uncomfortably through the hot sand. Glancing warily at Chigger, at his dirty brown hair that had not been washed for more than two weeks now, at the inflamed pimples on his face the mother wheeled sharply right, her son trailing dutifully behind, and moved thirty feet away before putting down the cooler.

Dropping his chairs, the little boy stepped eagerly into the inner tube, squirming to shift it up over his hips. But when he moved toward the surf his mother grabbed him by the arm, yanked him back, saying that he could not go into the ocean until she had put her bathing cap on. Instead of just putting the cap on, the mother towered over the boy, bent slightly at the waist, scolding him, like she was enjoying it. When the little boy started jumping up and down impatiently she cuffed him roughly across the top of the head so that he started crying.

The emptiness inside Chigger stirred. Slipping his hand into the pocket of his black raincoat again he wrapped his fingers around the revolver. If he shot the mother in the face would the little boy feel anything, maybe a sense of relief? Would he let out a whoop of joy, prance down to the sea finally free to do what he wanted, the shrill voice silenced now, simply a bad, slowly fading memory?

Sighing, Chigger shook his head regretfully. No, the little boy would not understand. He would probably just stand stunned; the mother having long since slapped the ability to feel out of him. Chigger grimaced; he certainly understood something about that, about having the ability to feel slapped out of him. The pain he remembered the most vividly was his mother slapping him, always slapping him. And, then, when he was sixteen, he had finally hit her back, hit her hard enough to break her jaw. And, then, the judge had put him in a juvenile detention center, locked him into the detention center where he stayed until he got his chance to run away and head for the coast, for the beach because his happiest memories were of trips to the beach.

When he was a child his mother used to drive him to the shore where he would sit alone all day playing in the sand, building castles with his bucket and shovel while she slept under the umbrella or ate. He would play in the sand or stare out at the sea feeling something good, feeling something he did not understand.

Suddenly, Chigger thought, "Maybe it would be better to shoot the kid, instead, put him out of his misery so that he doesn't grow up like me." Watching intently, he tried to make up his mind. They looked like cartoon characters, the rude mother still scolding while her flowers jiggled, the fat little boy still crying.

And no chance, Chigger shook his head sadly, no chance. They were both already too far gone, just piles of putty now slopping through life. They would go on that way until they finally dropped, just slopping through life. They would continue on, thinking everything was normal, thinking everything was on track despite the numbness, until the lights finally went out. Too far gone, the little boy was already too far gone. He had already been beaten to a pulp, his nerves endings dead so that he was just going through the motions, the slapping, the shrill voice a normal part of his existence.

Nothing there for Chigger, nothing real, no chance of getting feeling out of either the boy or his mother. They were just two more of the empty, wind-up dolls that filled his world. It would be a waste of bullets.

As Chigger walked away sand seeped into his black loafers, lodged beneath his heels. He wore no socks. He thought about taking the loafers off, walking barefoot but realized immediately that doing so would be cheating, that discomfort was part of it, that discomfort was the closest thing he had left to feeling. He was sweating heavily now under his long, black pants, black sweatshirt and black raincoat. His body was baking; he could feel moisture soaking into his sweatshirt. The discomfort felt good to him; it felt right.

On the other side of a ragged stone jetty that pointed like a finger out into the sea Chigger saw tanned bodies racing down the sand toward him, dodging beach blankets, throwing a football, One of the bodies skidded to a surf-splattering halt, stood frozen as Chigger approached. The young man, probably a junior or senior in high school, stood staring at something in his hand, something he had scooped out of the wash. Heavy, weightlifting muscles made him look clumsy as he bent over, sheltering what he had found with his other hand.

"Look," the athlete smiled, holding out a baby conch shell for Chigger to see.

"It's a conch shell," Chigger said.

"If I put it back do you think it will just wash up again?"

"I don't know."

Wading out through the churning surf to waist-deep water the fellow lowered the tiny, yellow shell carefully, watched it sink. When he straightened Chigger was still staring, causing him to laugh self-consciously. "Aren't you hot with all those clothes on?"

"Why should I be hot?" Chigger frowned.

"Your shoes are getting wet."

As he stood in the surf Chigger fingered the pistol in his raincoat pocket. If he shot this person he might get some feeling. Shoot the young stud in the chest then watch the expression of shocked disbelief on his face fade into gray death. Before Chigger could make up his mind, however, the young man charged off again scattering spray bullets, yelling for the ball.

Heat burned into Chigger's bare head, baked his shoulders through his layers of black clothing making the dizziness come back. Kneeling in the wash he cupped his hands together, splashed cool water onto his face tasting the saltiness on his lips. He did this several times, feeling water run down the back of his neck before standing and moving slowly on down the surf line ignoring the stares of sunbathers.

When he turned his face away to avoid the stares, looked out to sea, he saw a silent squadron of brown pelicans soaring low to the water. He counted six, their V of synchronized wings cranking down the waves. Brown against the wavering blue of the fiery afternoon sky, they dipped, gliding single file through a wave trough, barely skimming the surface, nearly encased in the falling wave curl but never caught. Chigger watched fascinated until they disappeared.

And he wondered what pelicans felt, knowing that it must be very pure, very peaceful. Only humans corrupted feelings; only humans killed their own feelings and the feelings of others, burying them under emotional garbage. When he reached the fishing pier it stood empty. He climbed the steep, wooden steps hanging carefully onto the railing. As he began walking out toward the sea end, however, a gap-toothed, potbelly wearing a tattered blue yacht captain's cap appeared from inside the bait shack.

"Ten dollars to fish," the potbelly stuck out a weathered paw.

"I'm not fishing. I'm just going out to look at the sea."

"Five dollars to watch them fish."

"There's nobody out there fishing."

"Five dollars to watch."

"Look, mister," Chigger said patiently, "I have a gun in my pocket. I came down to the beach today to kill somebody. Then, I'll probably kill myself. I just want to walk out to the end of the pier first, okay?"

Looking Chigger up and down, the potbelly spit a stream of reddish-brown tobacco juice over the railing. "I don't care if you have an atomic bomb in your pocket, boy. It's gonna cost you five dollars to watch."

With a shrug, Chigger turned to leave. When he had almost reached the bottom of the steps he felt suddenly dizzy and slipped, sliding down the last few stairs, scraping his back, driving splinters into his hand where he grabbed the rail. As he picked himself up he heard a cough. The potbelly was leaning on the railing above sneering down at him.

Walking under the pier, Chigger lowered his burning hand into a shallow pool of water where sand had been washed away from around the base of a piling. He heard the potbelly shuffle heavily across the planking overhead. He kept his hand submerged until it cooled, then leaned against the piling and picked at the splinters. The potbelly shuffled back, his bulk showing as a shadow through gaps between the planks. One sliver had run too deep to dig out with his nails. It was into the flesh. Forgetting his hand, Chigger looked around. The pier built a cool, pleasant cavern. He stirred the pool with the toe of his shoe.

"Hey!" Chigger did not respond.

"Hey! You under there! Under the pier!"

Leaning against the piling, Chigger stared out at the sea. When the shuffling above headed toward the stairs he moved to stand directly beneath them, pulled the pistol out of his pocket, cocked it, pointed it. Halfway down, the potbelly turned to find him, working in from the surf end until, suddenly, Chigger was there, right below him. The potbelly jerked, "Get out from under the pier!"
The potbelly had not seen the gun yet.

"You heard me, boy! I said get out from under there!"

Chigger just stared, his finger tightening on the trigger.

Suddenly, the potbelly's jaw dropped, "Jesus Christ, he does have a gun! What the hell!...I'm callin' the police!" Fright twisted the man's features. Grunting, he turned and tried to run back up the stairs, falling heavily as he neared the top. Chigger watched the potbelly struggle to stand, crawling, stumbling in his panic toward the bait shack. "Goddamn! Leave me alone! Get out from under there! I'm calling the police!" The bait shack door slammed shut.

The young man frowned, disappointed with himself. He had missed his chance. That had been his chance and he had missed it. What was he thinking; what was he waiting for? The potbelly had been scared, really scared. If Chigger had shot him in the gut he would have fallen down the rest of stairs blubbering raw fear. Then Chigger could have stood over him, pointing the pistol at his forehead, listening to him beg for mercy, listening to his anguish. He could have stood there for as long as he wanted taunting the potbelly who, despite the rot, was still capable of feeling fear, of feeling hate, of feeling something. And better yet, Chigger had felt a twinge himself. When he pointed the pistol at the potbelly's gut he had felt it, something deep inside, something animal; he had felt something. A more intense sensation was bound to have come from actually killing the man, from watching such a despicable slug die, from shooting the potbelly and watching him struggle with the nothingness he was sinking into.

As he walked out from under the pier Chigger suddenly noticed a small boy, maybe four or five years old wearing a yellow bathing suit, holding a yellow bucket in one hand and a red shovel in the other. The boy had been standing ten feet away, watching. "Is that a gun?" the boy asked.

"Yes, it is," Chigger nodded.

"Are you going to shoot that man?"

"Yes, I am."

"Why?"

The question startled Chigger. The child just stared, a totally open expression on his face, like he had asked, instead, why rain falls. Chigger sensed no fear in the boy, nothing like the potbelly's swirling, twisted currents. But, at the same time, Chigger sensed total awareness in the child. And Chigger realized that the little boy watching him was total awareness. He was freshness and newness. The child was feeling. And as Chigger watched, he understood immediately that the little boy was the one he had to kill. The little boy was the one. That was the answer. Instead of the potbelly Chigger had to shoot the little boy. The pain of killing such awareness, such freshness would be so unbearable for Chigger that it would make him feel something; so unbearable that it would make Chigger feel real again, if only for an instant.

The child was the one he had to kill.

"What is your name?" Chigger asked. The little boy did not answer.

"Why won't you tell me your name?" Chigger raised the pistol.

"Want to help me build a sand castle?"

"What?"

"A sand castle. I want to build a sand castle. My Mommy won't help me. My Mommy won't play."

Chigger lowered the pistol, "A sand castle." His shoulders slumped as he turned to look toward the lapping surf. He shook his head, stirring the dizziness again. The little boy was too much for him. This whole idea was too much for him. Chigger nodded his head slowly as the realization came that he had just been fooling himself. The entire afternoon had been a charade; only this time it had been his charade. He was not going to shoot the child. He was not going to shoot anybody. It was too late, much too late now for that. It was over.

A hunting pelican hovered out beyond the breaker line. It floated above the sea, then fell like a stone, a giant brown W of craning neck and folded wing to awkwardly splatter the surface. After its head reappeared the pelican floated gracefully with a fishtail sticking out of its bill. The bird seemed to be smiling.

Chigger asked, "Where is your mother?"

The little boy pointed up the beach with his red shovel.

"Do you know how to get back to her?"

The boy didn't answer.

"I think I hear her calling you to come back."
After cupping his hand behind his ear for a moment the boy shook his head, "I don't hear anything but the sea. Did you know that when you put a conch shell to your ear you can hear the sea?"

"Little boy, do you want me to shoot your mother for you?"

"No."

"I'm pretty sure I hear her calling. You'd better run back and check."

"Will you come with me, will you help me build a sand castle?"

Chigger shook his head, "No, little boy, it's too late for that. I can't help you build a sand castle. Now hurry back."

"I don't want to leave. I want to stay here. I want to stay here with you."

"You can't do that. You can't stay with me. You have to go back to your mother."

The child hesitated, staring at Chigger, his expression showing disappointment. Then, suddenly, he shrugged, smiled broadly, and ran off at full speed. As Chigger watched, the little boy began to skip, glancing back one time to wave with the red shovel.

As the sound of a police car siren rolled across the beach Chigger said quietly, "Goodbye, little boy." Then he squatted down. Time to go. He stuck the barrel of the pistol into his mouth. The steel tasted smooth, bitter against his tongue. When he looked, the pelican still floated out beyond the breakers, bobbing slightly with the swells. It was smiling at him. The pelican was riding the swells, a fishtail sticking out of its bill, smiling at him. Withdrawing the pistol barrel from his mouth, Chigger laid the weapon on the sand and dug a hole. When the hole felt deep enough he lowered the pistol in and buried it, smoothing the sand over first with his hands then, after standing up again, with the toe of his shoe so that the hole and the pistol no longer existed.

He drew a deep breath and, with that breath, finally felt something, something almost like peacefulness. As the siren grew louder he looked up the beach one more time but could not find the little boy. Then, still fully dressed, without hesitation, Chigger waded into the ocean, stepped through the line of low breaking waves, and began swimming awkwardly out toward the pelican.

ESSAYS

Teach the free Man, a review of Among Murderers: Life
After Prison
Charles Huckelbury:

> In the deserts of the heart
> Let the healing fountains start,
> In the prison of his days
> Teach the free man how to praise.
>   –W. H. Auden
>   In Memory of W. B. Yeats

The provocative title of Sabine Heinlein's book, Among
Murderers: Life After Prison, indicates she joined some
sort of commune of convicted killers or perhaps did
prison time herself. The reality is a series of interviews
with three men convicted of murder in New York and
eventually paroled. She is a journalist with an interest in
deviant behavior--specifically murder--and its effects on
the men who commit those crimes, the potential for
rehabilitating such men, and what to do with them once
they are released after serving decades in prison. The
subject remains an issue with profound social and
philosophical significance, one that demands the serious
and thoughtful attention that Heinlein brings to her work.
Her research extended from 2007 to 2011, during which
her awareness of the difficulties faced by former prisoners
and her insight into both their crimes and personalities
grew exponentially.

Ms. Heinlein's initial naiveté shows itself early when she
takes at face value one long-term prisoner's claim that
twenty years in prison had erased his memory of how to
turn on a kitchen faucet. Granted, prison facilities are
generally one-button affairs, but only someone on life
support could have trouble deciphering hot water from

cold. One of her research subjects (Angel) claims to have "fled in terror" from a supermarket when he discovered the multitude of brands of spaghetti sauce on the shelves. Heinlein also professes kinship with one of her subjects when she describes walking down the street with him: "Adam and I shared certain qualities. We were connected by a state of constant awareness. . . . Our vigilance protected us and kept us in check[.]" Anyone living in a large urban environment such as New York City should of course be aware, but to equate her response with the product of decades in prison indicates that she had at that point failed to comprehend the damage inflicted by prolonged incarceration. To her credit, her analysis improved.

Heinlein meets her research subjects at the Castle, a halfway house in New York City established by the Fortune Society and designed to assist former prisoners reentering society. The residents live on the premises while they look for employment and attend specific programs. Peripheral characters abound at the Castle, including Rich, a self-promoting narcissist who would be at home in one of Elmore Leonard's novels. These men provide an interesting cross-section of human foibles, but Heinlein doesn't allow them to distract her from her more serious work with the three men she has chosen for her study.

Adam is seventy-five years old and recently paroled after serving thirty-one years for the armed robbery of a theater, during which two people were killed. Adam did not shoot anyone, but he was found complicit in planning and executing the crime and sentenced accordingly. He expresses sincere remorse for his crime, describing how he was initially "haunted" in his prison cell by the specters of his victims. He maintains a pessimistic--some would say realistic--assessment of his future.

Heinlein's second subject is Bruce, paroled after twenty-four years for killing a man who harassed his girlfriend in a bar. Bruce is a product of the streets, where the code demands that anyone with a gun must be prepared to use it, and anyone who pulls a gun is obligated to shoot. Although living by the code sets him apart from conventional citizens, his guilt-ridden discussions of his crime indicate that he is not beyond redemption, a point Heinlein clearly makes. As Bruce tells her about guilt, "You gotta learn to carry it."

Angel is Heinlein's third subject and the least likeable of the three, perhaps explaining why his case occupies the most space. The product of a dysfunctional childhood, punctuated by a psychotic mother and no father, he strangled a sixteen-year-old girl when he was barely eighteen, finally earning parole after twenty-nine years and many denials. Angel persistently lies about his crime, ignoring his attempt to conceal the body. He falsely claims that he was in prison for another crime when questioned about the murder, to which he immediately confessed. He was actually arrested for the murder when police traced a ring removed from the dead girl and given by Angel to another. He never expresses remorse for his crime until a later parole hearing and only then because he was instructed by his attorney to do so. Asked by the parole board to name two things he would change about himself, he can think of none. Small wonder parole was long in coming.

One would have thought Heinlein would have done a little background study on the nature of her subjects' crimes, because that has an impact on the success of parole and obtaining employment and housing. And yet, she is surprised that Angel has lied to her about his crime. When asked about this prevarication, he tells her that he was "embarrassed because it was a girl." Then he would have been more forthcoming and not embarrassed had he killed a sixteen-year-old boy?

In attempting to understand Angel's pathology, Heinlein said, "He had detached himself from his former self." This is a significant error, especially considering that she had known Angel for only seven months at this time. Given his persistent lies, denials, and evasiveness, one could argue that Angel had not "detached himself" at all. His subsequent behavior revealed the person he had always been. This was not a detachment but an affirmation of who he was, his newly discovered devotion to Quaker nonviolence to the contrary. In perhaps the greatest demonstration of aberrant behavior, Angel decides to become, of all things, a Republican.

To her credit, Heinlein's understanding of her subjects and the criminal-justice system steadily grows with her experience. She chronicles Angel's repeated appearances before the parole board, describing the arbitrary nature of process, as opposed to the structured, objective assessment it purports to be. She describes required prison programming as "quackery," designed simply to do something and create staff positions. She learns "How removed [prisoners] are from our world" and comes to realize that "real rehabilitation could not be accomplished in prison." These insights reflect an inquiring, incisive mind's conclusions after examining the available evidence and bring to the public a needed corrective to the standard propaganda one finds in the twenty-four-hour news cycle.

Heinlein also replaces her unquestioned acceptance with a healthy skepticism for everything she hears, and her former attachment to her subjects gives way to reality: "Suddenly I felt separated from [Bruce] by a great distance." She was always separated from her research subjects; it simply took more experience and thought to acknowledge the fact.

Sabine Heinlein's book is an indispensable resource for anyone interested in understanding the effects of prolonged incarceration and the obstacles faced after decades in a cell. Citing the Quaker belief in the potential for change and the value of forgiveness, she cogently questions the possibility of disconnecting the past from the present. She concludes that "life--and murder--[are] far more complex and indecipherable than religion would have us believe."

More important, her work confirms Christopher Glazek's observation she cites, "Once you go to prison, you never really come back."

Orange Is The New Black Makes Me See Red
Erin George, 1141067

A confession: when I first heard about Piper Kerman's memoir, Orange Is The New Black, a few years ago, my initial reaction was, "Honey, spend some real time in a real prison and then come talk to me." Actually, being an inmate at a maximum-security prison for woman, myself, 'Honey' was not the word that I really used, but you get the idea. It wasn't until after the critically lauded Netflix series was produced that I actually got my hands on a copy of the memoir and read the story of a woman who served fifteen months in a minimum-security federal facility. I did so with the awareness that I wanted to evaluate it without bringing along the inevitable baggage that comes with any incarcerated person reading about another's experience. Kerman made that hard to do.

In itself, Orange Is The New Black falls somewhere in the middle of the memoir genre spectrum; while it is no Angela's Ashes, it is also several notches above Snooki's latest literary leaps. Kerman has an interesting enough story, but what really sells it is the hook. "It could have happened to me!" any member of her intended audience could reasonably think, enjoying the delicate shiver of a close call averted solely through his or her own splendid judgment and probity. Because Kerman's work is meant for people just like herself: well educated (as she never tires of telling us throughout the book, Kerman is the graduate of an "elite woman's college"), well off, and - most importantly – white.

Race appears to be almost an obsession with Kerman. She assiduously identifies the racial heritage of almost every person she encounters, taking great pains to contrast that with her own pale skin and, it seems, her conscious efforts to nobly overcome her natural tendency to fear said other races. Frankly, I'm surprised that she didn't whip out extensive genetic breakdowns for each character. Kerman self-identifies as a "random white girl," but slots everyone else into "tribes." You have the Puerto Ricans, the Dominicans, the Columbians, the African-Americans, and the Jamaicans, plus a smattering of other ethnic groups. But rather than using this attention to the racial diversity in the federal prison system for some constructive purpose, their presence is a tool used by Kerman merely to counterpoint her own precarious position as a gently-reared white girl ensnared in the cruel maw of the penal system.

Which brings me to my greatest problem with Orange Is The New Black. I'm all for inmates writing about their experiences. Not only is it therapeutic for someone who is inevitably traumatized in some way, but it also solidifies the fragile connections between existences inside and outside of prison walls. But I am dismayed to realize that this image of prison, exemplified by Kerman's multiple complaints about the lack of decent vegetables on the salad bar and pouts over the fact that she has to keep her pedicures a secret, is the image that the American public will glom onto as a typical prison experience. It is not.

There is no denying that it was unpleasant, to some degree. Just as summer camp is unpleasant to a lonely child. Seriously, though – on the continuum of prison experiences, Kerman's brief fifteen months was a sunny splash in the tide pools. Try falling off the edge of the continental shelf, as those women and men who are serving major sentences have done. They do not have access to a salad bar. Kerman's weekly visits with a loving, supportive partner would be an unattainable dream for most of them. To have a work assignment, as she did, building picnic tables outside on a lovely day next to a sparkling lake is a far cry from sweating it out in the dish window of a prison chow hall as most inmates have endured at some point.

Or try this: go into your bathroom and shut the door, turn off the light. Mentally spend just five minutes alone in an isolation cell, far from sunlight, fresh air, human voices and contact. Inhabit the closest approximation you are willing to endure of where thousands of American citizens molder every day. Now, change that amount of time to a year, ten years, twenty years, or more, and you get the barest glimpse of the reality of the forgotten souls in the Marianas Trench of our ostensibly humane incarceration system that is euphemistically and laughably referred to as "rehabilitative."

These are the most shameful secrets of our prisons that continue to go largely unregarded: the (mostly) men whose minds are crumbling away as surely as their physical health in the tiny cells tucked into the dankest corners of our prisons while the pretty and comfortable Piper Kerman bemoans the fact that, after a year or so in the Danbury, Connecticut federal facility, she is forced by the terms of her plea agreement to testify in a trial in Chicago and, as a result, has to spend time in a "real" jail where, for the first time, she is actually locked into a cell. And with another inmate, no less.

You can imagine my emotions upon reading that.

My fear is that Kerman's ephemeral moment within a wan imitation of lock-up is going to be the permanent view of the incarcerated held by the most smug, most influential segment of the American public, despite the fact that she could not be more atypical. Not because she is well educated, well off, and white. I share those characteristics as well. Kerman is atypical because her experiences barely reflect those of the majority of the real cogs in our nation's deplorable moneymaking prison machine. Society can barely fathom the difference between jail and prison, much less grasp the gradations between minimum-security fed time and a hard bid in a maximum-security penitentiary. But Kerman's work is one that the public can embrace. It's not too terrible to imagine (Nail polish! Salad bars!), just unpleasant enough. It is a safe, sanitized version of a truth that Americans simultaneously lust after and decry. We love our prisons, here in the old U.S. of A., but would rather not know how things get done behind the razor wire and stone walls. In Orange Is The New Black, Piper Kerman allows us to reconcile those tensions very neatly.

Do Prison and Punishment Deter Criminals from
Committing Crime?
Hakeem 7x. Butler

There is an interesting dynamic in the relationship
between crime, prison, and punishment; a dynamic that
speaks to the lifeblood of the twisted and wicked justice
system that is driven more by politics and economics than
anything else. Such a system is predicated by a "lock 'em
up and throw away the key" mentality. It is rarely about
correction and rehabilitation; it's geared more towards
oppression and repression. As a result of these forces, all
too many prisoners leave prison worse off than they were
when they entered the system. In many cases, the criminal
mind becomes more refined, sophisticated, and capable
of perpetrating advanced criminal behavior and activities.
The initial regret, remorse, and resentment a prisoner
may feel after they are imprisoned might spark thoughts
of redemption or repentance but once they get past that
stage, their old way of thinking is revamped.

The majority of people who commit crimes, do so
because it is a means to an end; a way to make fast cash to
support a habit or lifestyle. It is obvious that the crime
rate is more prevalent in impoverished communities,
communities that are undereducated and where the
unemployment rate is highest. You have to understand
that everyone has a common inclination to live
comfortably. Take a person who is uneducated, lacking
appropriate job skills, add to that a living environment
where crime and violence are commonplace: what is that
person's chances of getting involved in illegal activities?
Extremely high, right? I've spoken to prisoners who
honestly believe that selling drugs and being in "the game"
is all they know. They can't see themselves doing anything

else. So no matter how many times people like this get locked up and punished, their minds are not only transfixed on committing more criminal acts, they are also under the belief that they are pre-destined to be drug dealers or criminals – a belief that speaks volumes. Unless and until something drastic happens, the criminal lifestyle is their only reality. Mind you, one thing that is hard to change or correct is a twisted mind already made up. Prison and punishment can be assessed and analyzed in various ways. One view is that you have prisoners who are being punished by way of lengthy sentences. These overly harsh sentences cause prisoners to be bitter and make them feel like they need to take revenge on "the system" and on society in general. On the opposite side, you have some prisoners who have learned their lesson and want something better than a life of crime. Yet and still, the prisoners who have chosen the latter will reenter society with a felonious record that will keep them from landing a decent job; one that will allow them to support themselves and their families adequately. In this realm, one might be tempted or forced to commit another crime to earn a few extra bucks being that economics are synonymous with status. Once that demon is awake though, it is extremely hard to put back to sleep. So you do have prisoners who really had good intentions to leave the life of crime, only to get sucked back in. The cycle of recidivism is difficult to break. It has a lot to do with desperation and a lack of patience, which is a perilous mindset to have under any condition.

In essence, prison and punishment (no matter how harsh) are not tools that proof deterrent to sway criminals away from committing crimes. The high rate of recidivism substantiates this. In my opinion, it would have to take a psychological intervention to decriminalize a prisoner's mind because criminals who perpetually commit crimes are conditioned to do so. It is a learned activity and behavior that has to be seriously and diligently challenged in order to correct and change. The DOC does not tackle this aspect of criminal and violence prevention on a sincere level. On the surface it may appear that way, but beneath the surface, the correctional system only goes through the motions of treatment. I believe that the system does not really care if a prisoner changes or not. In fact, I had a high-level official tell me that he doesn't care if I go home and kill 100 people. I also had a "correctional" officer tell me that he wants me to go home and commit another crime so he would be able to send his kids to college. If I was a weak-minded individual, those authority figures would have lead me to believe that I could never amount to anything. The majority of prisoners are not strong-mind and that type of rhetoric would only reinforce the negative stereotypes that society and prisoners have of themselves.

In conclusion, prisons are designed to break prisoners psychologically. You can just imagine the low level of accountability and responsibility a mentally and emotionally damaged prisoner may have after years upon years of being oppressed and repressed. They would leave these places menaces to society, because they weren't reformed or rehabilitated effectively while here. So, in this vein, prison and punishment is not an effective tool to properly treat criminals in a realistic way. More often than not, the experience hardens deeply troubled prisoners. The choice of reform and rehabilitation depends solely on the individual. This individual has to be working with something truly special to defy the odds of never committing another crime again after being put in prison and punished for one. They would have to do a complete moral inventory of themselves to fully understand their place in life. Their self-excusing spirit

would have to be so great that it would create a whole new
way of thinking and behaving. This prisoner would have
to feel utterly tired of doing the same things over and over
and expecting different results. He or she would be so
tired of being counterproductive, irresponsible, lazy,
weak, and criminal-minded, that the person would be
catapulted in a new direction. This fresh state of
discontent would bring about a new way of doing things
and, as a result, a new person would be born; a person of
hope, remorse, compassion, love, care, responsibility,
purpose, faith, honor, respect, and decency. For I have
yet to meet a person in whom I did not see potential. We
all possess what we need to become our greatest selves.

PLAYS

The Monsters We Live With
Cassandra Fowler

This play is a series of short scenes between three
characters. Each scene occurs in a separate area of the
stage. A different actor should play the characters for each
area of the set. Actors may be dressed similarly to show
that they are playing the same character. The
manipulation of lighting should be used to draw attention
to different parts of the stage. During scene transitions,
the stage should be a series dimly lit of tableaus.

Lights go up center stage to reveal a tableaux.

Center stage, a semblance of a street sidewalk. Danny and
John stand in the middle of the sidewalk. Tableaux: John
stands stage left. He stands straight as if trying to appear as
absent from the moment as possible. He is clearly
consumed with an anger he is trying to suppress. He is
trying to listen, if only to understand. He glares down at
her. Danny stands with her feet wide apart as if she
stopped walking mid stride, or is trying desperately to
keep her balance. She looks down, clearly ashamed and
afraid. She seems to be melting under his gaze. This pose
is held for a moment.

She turns her head slightly outward, maintaining her gaze
at the ground.

D: I killed three people, and I'm not ashamed. I'm not
proud, and I'm 100% remorseful, but not ashamed. (She
raises her head to look at him, bravely, yet still afraid)

John stands center stage, holding a newspaper. He is the
only thing illuminated on the set. He reads aloud.

J: December 19th, the headline reads "Life in Prison comes to an End in the United States"

"After much discussion and political maneuvering, liberals in Congress have passed the defense of prisoners act, prohibiting life sentences for all crimes, with the exception of those outlined in the 'treasonous destruction clause'. Longtime opponent of the bill Marie Duquesne spoke yesterday on the passing of the bill:

"This is an insult to victims, American values, and to Lady Justice herself"

(Lifting his head to give his opinion)

I couldn't agree more. Disgusting.

Center stage again, the scene resumes

J: Then why did you lie about it? If you're not ashamed, why did you lie?

D: I couldn't tell you the truth. I wanted to, but I couldn't. We were so happy, and I was so happy for once. I didn't want to ruin it.

Daniela is a woman in her thirties, moderately good looking. She wears a white, cotton night gown that ends just below the knee; it, like her, is rather un-extraordinary. She sits on a twin sized bed with her knees bent, clutching a muslin doll. Somehow, the doll manages to be plainer than Daniela.

She speaks to the doll like a close friend

D: I met someone today at the courthouse. His name is
John. He was taking his niece to see it because she wants
to be a lawyer or something like that. Then, the girl, her
name is Sasha, (she mispronounces this) I think, walks up
to me and asks me what I do here, and then he came
over, and we started talking... you know...
Silence

D: We've been out a few times, and I think it's really
going good.
Silence

D: He calls me Danny, isn't that cute? Danny. Doesn't
that sound good? John and Danny. Like one of those TV
couples, right. I could see it. I would be like Lucy from I
Love Lucy, except not as stupid.

(She laughs as if with a group)

But no, think about it. I could be at home all day cooking,
and cleaning, with an apron, and he would come home
and

(Short Pause)

Well, I don't remember what they did after that,
(laughing) but you get it right?

This time the silence lasts longer. Much longer. Her
formerly happy composure sinks as she is reminded of
the reality of her situation.

(under her breath with a much sadder tone) You get it.

She rests her head on the doll's chest and sighs. She
closes her eyes as the lights dim.

A man, John, sits on an elegant green sofa. Across from him sits his therapist, a middle aged man clinging to what few hairs remained on his otherwise shiny head. John is dressed in the sort of clothing that passes for casual among the very rich, but which any other person would describe as fancy.

J: (noticeably agitated) I really don't understand. How did I not see it? I mean, is there something I missed? Was there some glaring red sign that I should have picked up on?

Therapist: Why don't you tell me what you think? What was it that first attracted you to her?

J: Well, I don't know. I guess, she just seemed different. (He grows calm as he continues to talk) I mean, I saw her walk by that day, in the courthouse and she just looked so different. Everyone was milling about, complaining about the rain, about the traffic, or what have you. Everyone except her. She just looked... I don't know... lost I guess. Not like she didn't know where she was, but that she didn't know where she was going, in life I mean. She didn't walk so swiftly or so confidently. It seemed as if she were sitting back and thinking while her body moved her about. I guess I was curious.

Therapist: You were curious about why she was lost?

J: Not why she was lost, but why she was here. You don't typically see that sort of person in a courthouse. She was so light, if you know what I mean. It was as if she was hardly there. It was a refreshing break from the strong characters that we had seen all day.

Therapist: And after you talked to her, did she still seem "light" as you say

J: (leaning back) Yeah. I mean, she hardly spoke. She told me she was here to see her sister in court. I just assumed her sister was a lawyer or something. I assumed her sister was actually her sister, not some old prison friend. (this last line is said with a bit of disgust)

Therapist: So you liked her because she was reserved. That seems reasonable enough to me. How could you have known what she had done? After all, she hardly sounds like the type.

J: (more to himself than the therapist) The type? Ha. People only really have one type. The good natured kind that sometimes slips up, but ultimately is trying to do the right thing. She doesn't exactly fit that description, does she?

Therapist: I suppose not.

J: Monsters have types. I didn't think so before. I just assumed they were all of the fire breathing variety. But not this one. She's the type that hides under the bed and convinces you that she is just a shadow, that her breath on your neck is just a draft from the window. You get lulled to sleep. (His voice grows quieter as he says this line) Silence.

Therapist: And what next? What does the monster do when you're asleep.

J: It climbs into bed with you, and cries.

Return to center stage.

J: You didn't want to ruin it, so you lied? I was happy too Danny! I was happy, and now I feel like an idiot! You let me believe that this was real, that I knew you. And now you want me to believe you're a good person, that you're reformed? You're selfish Danny! And a liar!

D: I lied because I knew you couldn't handle it. You're jump to conclusions without thinking.
Sometime shortly after they had just met, Daniela and John are walking together and engaging in casual conversation.

Danny wears a pale blue floral printed dress that looks appropriate for a 1950's tea-party in both style and modesty. Her thin waist clearly accentuated, Danny is a picture of domesticity, despite her particularly lonely home life. She has attempted a small heel for the event, although it is clear from the style of the heel (closed-toed with a rounded toe, a poor choice for the occasion) that she has not worn heels for a while. She walks slowly and deliberately, which John mistakes for feminine timidity, a quality he finds rarely in women today. John's clothing is also exemplary, yet his dress is a product of habit. With the exception of the grey fedora he decided to wear, his judgment clearly impaired by his nerves, John is the poster child for the modern man, with just a hint of chauvinism.

The awkwardness of the scene should make it clear that this is one of their first encounters. Both are nervous, Daniela moreso than John, and searching for the right topic of conversation.

J: I love this part of town. Not many people know about it, so it's not busy like the rest of the city. Everyone's really friendly and you get to know the people working in

the shops and what not. It really is one of the best parts of
the city.

D: (quietly, trying to come up with a response) Yeah...
it's... quiet... nice

J: Yeah. I grew up in the area, so I'm familiar with all the
lesser known places. When I was a kid I would come
down here all the time and just sit in the square reading.
(He sees that she is uninterested, despite her efforts to
seem engaged)... What about you? Did you grow up
around here?

D: No. Well, I'm from the city, but the other side, like
near the river.

J: Is your family still in the area?

D: No, I don't really have any family. (Catching her
mistake, she quickly corrects it) Well, except my sister.
But I don't really see her much.

J: The one at the courthouse right, what's that like, having
family in the justice world? (he says this like a joke,
chuckling towards the end)

D: (she smiles shyly, she laughs lightly to be polite, though
the real concern soon becomes very clear) Yeah, it's
interesting. You really learn a lot about the whole system.
It's a lot different from what you think when you're a kid.

J: I can imagine. Much grittier in real life, I guess.

D: Yeah. But not how you would expect. It's really
separate from everything real. You start off waiting for
something to change, for someone to realize the truth, to

look at you and see that you're not a criminal, that you just slipped up. After a while you realize that what you are hoping for is a miracle. Then you realize that miracles don't happen, not in real life.

J: (seriously contemplating her words, while trying to find something to contribute) I suppose destitution is an apt word for the average prisoner. But that's rather the point of prison, isn't it? To make one's suffering equal to the suffering they impose on others. It's penance.

D: (not realizing the boldness of her words) Do you suffer for the suffering you caused?

J: (shocked and slightly taken aback) No. I don't think I have caused such great suffering. (Regaining his composure) It's a matter of degree.

She shrugs, looking away. Clearly she is not impressed by the answer.

J: I think the little pain I cause by jay-walking is nothing compared to the rapists and murderers in prison. As far as I can tell, they got themselves there.

She can't help but chuckle at John's unfamiliarity with crime.

J: (relieved that the tension has been lifted, he smiles) what? Did I say something wrong?

D: No, no. It's just... Jay-walking? That's the best you could come up with? (Outright laughter) Is that the worst thing you've ever done?

J: (He laughs to, deciding to play along) Well excuse me! I'm not expert in crime!

D: Apparently not!

The laughter subsides. John, assessing this conversation as a success, is thoroughly pleased with himself. As with any hopeless romantic, he feels the need to give an evaluation Danny.

J: You know, you're strange.

D: (not sure if this is a compliment, she asks meekly) Strange?

J: Yes. Very abnormal. (It is his turn to be mysterious) I like it.

John sits in his therapist's office, as before. He has just recounted the previous scene to his therapist. Much in contrast to the previous scene, John's posture is much less confident. He appears defeated and confused.

J: I keep going back over that moment. I've never been very religious, but I wonder if this is all some sort of penance. Am I paying for some sin now?

Therapist: Have you considered that what she said that day may have been her trying to tell you something?

J: What, that she's a criminal? That prison was just so damn sad and she was so damn alone?
Lights go up upstage to reveal Danny in her bedroom, hugging her cell buddy and crying the day of the previous scene. She is wearing the same pale blue dress. Lights go down in Danny's corner of the stage.

J: (voice tainted with disgust) As if she didn't deserve it.
Therapist: Then why does it bother you so much, this loneliness?

J: It's what she said. That waiting. It's like what I'm doing now, waiting.

Therapist: What are you waiting for, John?

J: To wake up. Or to forget. I don't know, just something.

Therapist: So you are bothered because you can sympathize with someone who you describe as a monster.

J: Sympathize? No. She deserved it, I didn't. Empathize. I guess I can empathize.

Therapist: Do you really think your pain is comparable?

J: No. That's the worst part. It must have been so much worse for her.

Lights go up on Danny's bedroom again. She has just stopped crying. She lies still, breathing heavily with her arms wrapped around her doll.

J: But I don't feel sorry. The sad thing is, I was happy. I was so happy.

On a similar street corner, the two are comfortably speaking with each other. It is clear they are both deeply infatuated with each other, but have lost the awkwardness of first dates.

J: So, are you going to tell me?

D: Tell you what?

J: Oh you know. That secret you've been subtly keeping since the day we met.

D: (she looks at him, confused and slightly fearful)

J: (Pausing playfully) Where are you from?

D: (laughing) That's it? Where am I from?

J: Of course

D: (jokingly) I thought you had found out something about me.

J: Is there something I should know?

D: Possibly... you'll find out.

J: Very cute. And clever. You've managed to avoid answering the question again!

D: I'm not avoiding it! I –

J: Then answer the question!

D: I'm from the Southside of town. Near the river.

(John is silent for a moment as if waiting for more)

D: What? I answered the question.

(Silence)

D: What, don't you believe me?

D: What do you feel sorry for me?

John has by now realized that being silent is the best way
to get her to talk

D: You know, it wasn't as bad as people make it seem.
Yeah, there's a lot of stuff that happens there, but it's not
like a war zone or anything. People aren't just shooting
people or getting shot. They do other things too.
And they always have a reason for doing bad things.
Maybe not a good reason, but they have a reason.

(More silence)

D: What?

J: hmmm

D: Hmmm. What does hmmm mean?

J: It doesn't mean anything.

D: You're always hmmm-ing at me. It means something.

J: how about 'Hmmm was that so hard?'

D: You're ridiculous

Their chatter continues a few moments longer, and then
dies down. They freeze in place as lights fade on them.

John sits in his armchair talking with his therapist. Daniela
sits on her bed in her white nightgown.

J: I can remember it word for word now. I keep reading over it looking for a mistake.

D: It was so simple, the way they said it. They just summed me up in a few sentences.

They recite the article in unison.

"At 11:59 am, convicted felon Daniela Cole is released from prison. Cole was serving a life sentence for multiple homicides when her sentence was reduced to 10 years under the Reasonable Sentencing Act. Her Correctional Officers claim she is perfectly reformed, but many are skeptical."

D: And that was it. I was just the first story they had about that law.

J: That simple. They just summed it all up like that, as if it was over now.

Center stage again.

J: (not impressed by Danny's attempts at defiance) I don't feel sorry for you. You deserved to suffer.

T: You don't have to feel sympathy, John. Just try to listen, if only to understand.

D: (somewhat pleadingly) I did suffer, John! I did. You don't know what it's like, to be trapped like that. No visitors, no friends. You're lucky if you have people who tolerate you!

J: (unable to listen any longer) I don't care! I don't care about how lonely you were, or how sad you were, or how no one loved you! You got yourself there.

D: (suddenly enraged, and unable to be ashamed any longer, she screams back) Okay! I know, I got myself there, and I know I deserved it. And everyone thinks I should have rotted away and died in there. But I didn't! I'm still here John; I still exist.

(Calming down, pause)

T: Try and look at it from her perspective.
By this point, John is the one looking down while she looks intently at him.

D: I did a horrible thing, and I was punished for it. I punished myself for it. But I can't keep suffering for it. I can't.

John stands, holding a newspaper. The tableaus in the other parts of the set are dimly lit, but still visible. He reads aloud.

J: March 3rd, the headline reads "First lifer released from prison after Reasonable Sentencing Act"

He closes the paper without reading the rest.

J: Disgusting. To think some hardened criminal will be walking the streets soon.

Center stage again

J: (After a pause. He says quietly) And I don't want you to
suffer. Not anymore. (Raising his head to meet her gaze)

But I won't be sorry that you did.

They look at each other, exhausted from their argument.
Neither is sure what to expect next. They are caught
between hope, anger, and resignation.

All tableaus are illuminated. Curtains Close

The Dayroom Club
Patricia Prewitt

SETTING: Modern day dayroom of a women's prison. There are two or three small tables and several chairs. Bathroom/showers are alluded to up right off stage. Rotunda [all exits from housing unit go though rotunda] is alluded to down right off stage. Cells are alluded to behind backdrop up left off stage. Imaginary phone [chair] is on edge of stage center left. No actors on stage for opening.

CAST: (in order of appearance) Loud Speaker announcer (off stage), Snarky Girl AKA Mickie, Old Lifer AKA Patty, Child Custody AKA Bird, Gossip Girl AKA Amy, Late Girl AKA Glennis, and an assortment of others named and unnamed.

ACT I:

LOUD SPEAKER: COUNT CLEAR. COUNT CLEAR. DAYROOMS ARE OPEN. DAYROOMS ARE OPEN. [Old Lifer and Snarky Girl and a few others enter with balls of yarn, crochet hooks, messy pot holder project, cups of coffee and sit at a table at center left.]

SNARKY GIRL: Wonder what that count was all about right here in the middle of the afternoon?

OLD LIFER: Probably found a gate open somewhere. Now, Mickie, don't worry. I told you that I'd teach you to crochet, and I will. Relax.

SNARKY GIRL: It may not be as easy as you think. I'm
not crafty, but I've always wanted to learn. I shoulda
learned in the 80's during one of my earlier bits, but—
[loudspeaker interrupts]

LOUD SPEAKER: LINE UP FOR SMOKE BREAK.
LINE UP ON YOUR LEVEL. IF YOU LIVE
UPSTAIRS, LINE UP UPSTAIRS. [always repeats]
LINE UP FOR SMOKE BREAK. LINE UP ON
YOUR LEVEL. IF YOU LIVE UPSTAIRS, LINE UP
UPSTAIRS. [Girls enter up left grumbling or anxious,
fooling with pouches, packs and lighters and line up
across the stage.]

LOUD SPEAKER: JONES. MARSHA JONES. 1-1-3-4-
5-6-8-2. COME TO THE ROTUNDA. IN FULL
GREYS. JONES. MARSHA JONES. 1-1-3-4-5-6-8-2.
COME TO THE ROTUNDA. IN FULL GREYS.

CHILD SUPPORT GIRL: [enters hurriedly holding a
legal letter and envelope] Miss Patty, I need your help. I
got this legal letter... last night. [Old Lifer starts reading
while Bird babbles] It's about child support for my little
girls. They are with their daddy's mommas right now. In
separate towns, and the families are taking care of them
cause I'm in here, but scared they wanna take them away
from me. Forever. Adopt them. They've talked about it!
And right now they won't even take collect calls. I can't
but minutes... until state pays hits and they may not even
take my calls then—

OLD LIFER: [interrupts] Bird, you owe over seven
thousand dollars in child support and they want to take
your prison pay—

CHILD SUPPORT GIRL: [interrupts dramatically] I only get seven fifty a month until my GED results get back, if I pass...

OLD LIFER: [encouragingly] And you will... you have.

CHILD SUPPORT GIRL: Ya get just a dollar more a month if you get you GED, so I'll makes a whopping eight fifty. Bit I'm gonna try to get on at the sewing factory... Even then I'll never pay back seven thousand dollars! NEVER. Hey, Mickis, you work there, what's the starting pay at the factory?

SNARKY GIRL: Thirty cents an hour. Top pay is seventy-one cents, but it will be a while before you get to that. If ever. [Bird slumps.]

LOUD SPEAKER: JONES. MARSHA JONES. COME TO THE ROTUNDA IN FULL GREYS. JONES.

OLD LIFER: Let's write a letter—

CHILD SUPPORT GIRL: [interrupts] Seven thousand dollars? Are you freaking serious? The sewing factory pays thirty cents? What's that a month?

OLD LIFER: Let's see. On a good day, it's six hours? I mean a day without extraneous counts or fire drills, and you don't get paid for the lunch break. Six times thirty cents is a dollar eighty a day. Five days a week is nine dollars a week. For, let's say four weeks, nine time times four is thirty-six. It's roughly thirty-six dollars a month. Thank God you don't smoke! But you do have to budget in your necessities: Toothpaste, toothbrush, shampoo. All your hygienes. And I know you'd love to save up for a pair of tennis shoes so that you could get out of those hard state boots. And a t-shirt so you wouldn't have to wear that polyester uniform top all the time...

CHILD SUPPORT GIRL: [moans] Seven thousand dollars...

SNARKY GIRL: That's what happens when your people get on welfare. Somebody gotta pay. [all throw her dirty looks] You all know I'm right!

LOUD SPEAKER: JONES. JONES, MARSHA. COME TO THE ROTUNDA IN FULL GREYS. YOU HAVE A VISIT!

ALL: BLUE! YA GOTTA VISIT! CAN"T YOU HEAR EM?

VISIT GIRL: [enters] I HEAR EM! HAD TA PUT MY SHOES ON, FOR CRYING OUT LOUD! [rushes past smokers]

ALL: Have a good visit! [Blue smiles and gives thumbs up]

SMOKER 1: So I TOLD HER, "Keep my name outta yo mouth, bitch!"

SMOKER 2: Girl, you be trippin'!

SMOKER MOOCH: Gotta extra roll-up? I'll pay you back. Promise. My grandma is putting some money on my books when her check comes in.

SNARKY GIRL: That's what they always say.

SMOKER 4: [patting herself feverishly] Where's my lighter? Somebody steal my freakin' lighter! [doubles back]

SMOKER 5: Let's do something special for her birthday; she'll never expect it.

SMOKER 6: This is going to be awesome. I'll make some fudge like Water Baby taught me—with sugar cubes and peanut butter.

SMOKER 5: It'll surprise the shit out of her. I got a Hershey bar I been saving that we can melt on top! Yum! But, can you keep it in your locker, so I don't eat it?

SMOKER 6: Sure, but who's gonna watch me?

ACT II:

LOUD SPEAKER: SMOKE BREAK! QUIET IN THE ROTUNDA. NO STRAGGLERS. SMOKE BREAK! [girls cross down to exit stage]

SMOKER 7: Never could get along with that dick parole officer. One time he called me in and—

SMOKER 8: [interrupts loud and joyful] I LOVE SATURDAYS! OFF WORK! YEAH!

SMOKER 4: [catching up] It was in my other shirt. I found it! Good thing. I'd hate ta havta beat a bitch down. [Smokers file off stage chattering. As the last one touches the tile, Late Girl runs across pulling on her coat.]

SMOKER 8: [shaking head at Smoker 4] Whatever...

COUGHER GIRL: [hacking coughing] They are killing me. I gotta quit! [she coughs all exits and entrances]

LATE GIRL: [pulling on coat] WAIT! HEY, DON'T LET THAT DOOR CLOSE BEHIND YOU! HEY! WAIT!

OLD LIFER: Bird, do you have any other letters from the state about child support and custody?

CHILD SUPORT GIRL: Yeah, I think, let me look in my footlocker... [exits quickly]

GOSSIP GIRL: Trips me how much Bird has grown. I know where she comes from, her family. Hell. That had the girl cookin' dope before she was in high school. Pretty cool to see her trying so many new things. Trips me out. Patty, you're a big part of that. She looks up to you.

OLD LIFER: I'm really proud of Bird, but it's not me. She's a special kid.

SNARKY GIRL: I heard that she'd never even read a book until she got locked up.

GOSSIP GIRL: She's come a long way. Her people are hardcore redneck racists, like neo-Nazis. [quickly] Here she comes.

CHILD SUPPORT GIRL: [reenters and plops down] This is all I got.

OLD LIFER: We were just talking about you, Bird. [Gossip Girl looks shocked, afraid that Patty is going to tell the bad things she told about Bird's family, but smiles wen she realizes her secrets are safe.] We're proud of your accomplishments and how much you've grown as a person. I know you've got that GED in the bag. You joined both theatre and poetry classes. You're reading important books and really thinking...

CHILD SUPPORT GIRL: Those Holocaust books got me to thinking about all the lies I've been told. I don't want to be part of hateful thinking anymore.

OLD LIFER: You're a seeker Bird. That's what Father Behan would call you. A seeker. You're searching for the truth. And Bird is a perfect name for you. You're soaring now and have raised your perspective to a more lofty one. From way high. [pats Bird's shoulder smiling]

CHILD SUPPORT GIRL: What does that mean? Perspective?

OLD LIFER: I love that you are not afraid to ask questions. Perspective is your point of view, how you look at things. Climb up on the roof and look down. You'll see things from a different perspective.

SNARKY GIRL: Yeah, like they'd shoot you down!

OLD LIFER: Bad analogy. Are you on a top bunk? [Bird nods] Doesn't the room look different from up there than it does from a bottom bunk? [Bird nods] My view of prison was way different before I came in. I was scared to death of the bad girls I'd run up against in prison.

GOSSIP GIRL: I was scared, too. Just a kid my first time! The girls in county really yanked my chain and had me expecting the worst. I thought I'd be fighting all the time. [demonstrates a move]

OLD LIFER: Exactly... but when I got here, I realized that we inmates are no different than any other women. We come in all sizes, shapes, colors, temperaments, backgrounds... But at the end of the day, we just want to love and be loved.

SNARKY GIRL: Don't forget to throw in a few hot meals, too.

EAR HUSTLE GIRL: And a lumpless mattress! Feels like I'm sleeping on a pile of rocks. [puts hand on lower back as if in pain]

EAR HUSTLE GIRL 2: I could do with some love, alright. Some real lovin', some Tatum Channing lovin'!

ALL: Woo hoo! [Chime in with agreeable words and other men's names. Everyone gets a bit wild and loud talking at the same time.] "I'll take Brad Pitt! I'd give Angelina a run for her money." "Me, too, but not the way you mean!" "Give me the Antonia Banderas, ya know, Desparado?" "George Clooney beats them all. " "I know he's an old guy, but I've always had a thing for Sean Connery, 007." "The lead singer for Nickelback!" "Denzel Friggin Washington! Training Day? Now there's a man!"

DAYROOM GIRL: Tatum Channing beats em all! Did you see that Magic Mike movie? About the male strippers? I saw it before I came in. Wooee! Did they show it here?

GOSSIP GIRL: No, we'll never see it. We can't see anything but G and PG.

SNARKY GIRL: You'd never guess that this is an "adult institution" by the cartoons they show us. [to Patty] Does this look right? [shows tangled mess to lifer]

[Shower Girl enters with towel on head and shower gear.]

SHOWER GIRL 1: SOMEBODY LEFT THEIR DRAWERS IN SHOWER FOUR!

ALL: AMY! [drawn out and pronounced Aye-Mee]

SHOWER GIRL 1: Good God! That shower's so friggin cold, I froze my ass off!

SNARKY GIRL: Not all of it. [Dirty looks between them as Shower Girl shivers off.]

LOUD SPEAKER: ALL LOST SOULS BIBLE STUDY TO THE CHAPEL. ALL LOST SOULS BIBLE STUDY TO THE CHAPEL.

OLD LIFER: [to Snarky Girl] That looks awful, Mick. Rip it out.

SNARKY GIRL: [aghast] Are you serious? Looks good to me.

CHURCH GIRL: [a couple of girls with Bibles cross downstage.] THEY CALLED CHAPEL! COME ON, TRACY! [looks back impatiently]

COUGHER GIRL: [coughs back upstage] I gotta quit.

CHURCH GIRL: I'M NOT WAITING, TRACE! SEE YOU THERE... MAYBE!

[When they straggle back from smoking, one girl sits down at a table and the other girl braids her hair. When Smoke Breaks are called, these two always go out to smoke, then come back to work on their hair. If there is room on the stage, some can play cards, too.]

LOUD SPEAKER: TEN MINITE INSIE RECREATION MOVEMENT! INSIDE RECREATION. [A few girls cross stage to catch the movement,]

OLD LIFER: [to girl passing through to Rec] Hey, Lori, what did Medical do for you?

REC GIRL: Just what we thought. Gave me a box of generic sinus pills and told me to drink more water... for my knee. [Everyone snickers knowingly. Rec Girl limps off.]

EAR HUSTLE GIRL: I got the same sinus pills and advice for my gall bladder.

EAR HUSTLE GIRL 2: That's what they gave me for my acid reflux.

SNARKY GIRL: I'll probably get sinus pills for this leg!

OLD LIFER: [to Child Custody] Let's sort these out by date. You, [to snarky] unravel that and start over. I'm not kidding, Mickie. You have to concentrate. I've taught thousands of girls to crochet, and I know you can learn, but you gotta follow directions and focus. Fo-cus.

SNARKY GIRL: What? Can't you save part of this? [negative glance from Lifer] Hey, do we go to the store on Monday or Tuesday this week?

OLD LIFER: FOCUS! Focus on your stitches, Mick!

GOSSIP GIRL: Tuesday. We spend on Tuesday.

SNARKY GIRL: Thanks. It's hard to get a straight answer around here. [To Lifer] And I am focusing. I can chain and think about other stuff.

OLD LIFER: I can't tell.

LOUD SPEAKER: AA IS CANCELED. AA IS CANCELLED.

ONE OR MORE GIRLS: [whoop] HALLELUJAH! [or something like it]

LATE GIRL: [enters to ask] What did they say?

SNARKY GIRL: Na AA. Nada. Not happening. Go lay down. [Late Girl exits]

OLD LIFER: [to Visit Girl coming back through] Hi, Blue! Bid you have a good visit?

VISIT GIRL: Yes...no... [fighting back tears] My baby is calling that lady mommy. She cried when I tried to hold her and wouldn't even sit on my lap. It was awful. She hardly snows me.

SNARKY GIRL: She doesn't know you. How long has it been? A year or more? What do you expect? [everyone on stage gives her dirty looks] I'm just saying...

VISIT GIRL: She'll be five when I get out. Five. I really screwed up when I hooked up with Darrel Friggin

Hughes. But you couldn't have told me that back then. I thought the sun rose and set in his hazel eyes. My momma always told me not to trust a black man with light eyes. That son-of-a-bitch got off with probation. And he has a record a mile long. Put the whole case on me. [exits mumbling]

LOUD SPEAKER: RECREATION MOVEMENT IS CLOSED. REC MOVEMENT IS CLOSED.

GOSSIP GIRL: [back from spoke break] Guess what I just heard. Amanda and Trina went to the hole! Just this afternoon.

OLD LIFER: What for?

GOSSIP GIRL: I don't know yet, but I'll get the scoop on the next smoke break. I bet it was over that Jay Jay thing, you know, from before... Or it could be cause Amanda's putting money on Trina's books. It could be something bout that. Manda's from my area. Can't trust any of her people. Her older brother is the worst. [pause] Don't tell her I said that, cause her people are mean as snakes. You know?

OLD LIFER: No...

ACT III:

LOUD SPEAKER: LIBRARY. TEN MINUTE LIBRARY MOVEMENT. LIBRARY MOVEMENT.

[girls scurry across the stage with books]

LIBRARY GIRL 1: Hurry, they only let the first 10 in! I need a book BAD! I've been here so damned long that I've read all the good books at least once.

LIBRARY GIRL 2: Girl, you've only been here since September...

LIBRARY GIRL 1: Seems longer. Lots longer...

LIBRARY GIRL 3: I heard she had butter stashed in a plastic glove and got busted right outside the chow hall.

LIBRARY GIRL 4: What an idiot. I keeps my butta in my bank! [pats bosom, exit all]

LIBRARY GIRL 3: And her girlfriend had the potato! They both was busted! Hurry! [Library girls exit quickly]

PHONE GIRL 1: [on side of stage with hand and finger simulating a telephone] [everyone on stage listens] I can't call her. Her man won't take collect calls and I can't afford minutes right now. Not until state pay. Try to find out for me, please. And tell her I love her and I'm sorry not to be there when she needs me most. I'll call you tomorrow. Yeah. Thank you so much for taking my calls. I love you, Sis. Bye. [hangs up]

PHONE GIRL 1: [turns to Old Lifer] It's the diabetes. My sister says they may have to amputate her leg.

OLD LIFER: Oh my God. I'm so sorry, Theresa. How old is your momma?

PHONE GIRL 1: She's not even 50 yet! And my sister is bearing the brunt of all this since I'm stuck in here and absolutely useless to Mom and the rest of the family. My little brother's doing a dime in Leavenworth. My sister is the only one of us who's straight arrow. A good kid. [pause] What's momma gonna do without her leg?

SNARKY GIRL: [interjects] I'm afraid I'm gonna lose my leg. Look at this know. Feel it. It's serious. That nurse at sick call just blew me off. Said it was nothing. Feel it. Go on, feel it... Here... [Phone Girl ignores Snarky and exits]

 LOUD SPEAKER: LIBRARY MOVEMENT IS CLOSED. LIBRARY MOVEMENT IS CLOSED.

LATE GIRL: Late Girl holding books stops dead in her tracks on stage] Man! Can't a girl pee around here without missing out? Kiss my [lily white or big black] ass! [exits]

BATHROOM GIRL: [enters from side screaming] WHICH ONE OF YOU TRIFLIN' HOES LEFT ALL THOSE NOODLES IN THE FIRST SINK? THERE'S ENOUGH TO FEED A FAMILY A FIVE! IF I CATCH THAT NASTY COW... [to all] CLEAN UP AFTER YOURSELVES. AIN'T NO RICH PRINCESSES UP IN HERE. NAST ASS...

SNARKY GIRL: [chuckles] That never gets old!

BATHROOM GIRL: [starts to exit, then turns back to announce] AND SOMEBODY LEFT THEIR SOAP ON SINK 3! [exits in a huff]

ALL: AMY!

GOSSIP GIRL: [enters form smoke break with a group—excited] Miss Patty, I got the four-one-one! Manda was calling Trina's trick, behind her back, and trying to get him to put money on her books and Trina found out! He told her, of course! And so she confronted Manda and BAM! Tall Ashley on C-wing said black Linda at the library told her all about it.

OLD LIFER: Did they physically fight?

GOSSIP GIRL: No, they yelled a lot... enough to get the people's attention. You know how loud they are.

OLD LIFER: Be right back. Gotta check my laundry. [Exits UR] [girls cross back with books from library]

PROUD GRANDMA: [enters with crocheted item] Look what I made for my granddaughter! It took me forever! Hope she like it!

ALL: [variations of:] Ah, Faye, how cute. She's gonna love that!

SNARKY GIRL: I could make one, too, if Miss Patty would quit screwing around and teach me how. [everyone ignores this statement]

PROUD GRANDMA: How many stamps do you think it'll take to mail it out? I have four.

OLD LIFER: [enters with folded laundry and sits it on the table while she sits back down to sort letters] I bet it will take eight. Recently I sent out some slippers about that size and weight.

STAMP GIRL 1: I have two I can spare.

STAMP GIRL 2: I have a couple, too.

PROUD GRANDMA: Thanks so much! You're lifesavers! Promise I'll pay you back next week on canteen day. [starts to exit]

CHILD CUSTODY GIRL: Miss Faye, did you get your answer from the parole board yet? It's been awhile since you saw them.

PROUD GRANDMA: Yeah, got it Thursday... but I couldn't talk about it. [deep breath] Got a 5-year setback. [That gets everyone's attention. The girls stop what they are doing and stare at her.]

CHILD CUSTODY GIRL: Wow! Five whole years until you get another chance? Another hearing?

SNARKY GIRL: I'll be back here twice in that time! [snorts to herself] I'm doing life on the installment plan.

PROUD GRANDMA: [to Snarky] You sure are! [to all] At my hearing, the Parole Board told me that I was doing great. No conduct violations. Took all the classes they told me to. A "model inmate". [uses fingers to show quotation marks] They told me to keep up the good work. Then they slam me with a 5-year setback? I haven't told Mom or the kids yet. They had such high hopes. Mom is afraid she won't live to see me come home. She's just hanging on... so sick, but five more years... I don't know. My grandkids are growing fast. I don't know... [exits]

SNARKY GIRL: I am doing life on the installment plan, but the truth is, I do good in here. I need structure, I guess. In here, I am somebody. I get respect. Out there, I'm just another skanky drug whore. [jokes:] I'm not a crack whore, cause I'll do any kinda drug.

[introspectively] Inside, I'm not nobody. When they let me out, I have no place to go, no job skills... And I go back to the only life I know. The streets. Stealing. Shooting up. [pause] At least in here I have three hots and a cot. [chuckles] And all you crazy friends. [Miss Patty squeezes her shoulder in sympathy. Her words make everyone else uncomfortable—too close to the bone.]

LOUD SPEAKER: EXTRA DUTY, EXTRA DUTY. IF YOU HAVE EXTRA DUTY COME TO THE ROTUNDA WITH YOUR COAT AND EXTRA DUTY SHEET. [Girls run across stage with pink ED sheets pulling on coats. All but one return quickly.]

LATE GIRL: [enters] What did they say?

SNARKY GIRL; [pronounces slowly and snidely] Ex-tra Du-ty. Clean out your ears, girl. Need a Q-Tip?

CHILD CUSTODY GIRL: [to Snarky] Mickie, do you have kids?

SNARKY GIRL: [sadly] Yeah.

CHILD CUSTODY GIRL: What about em? Where are they?

SNARKY GIRL: They're all big now. One's in federal. Not sure where right now. I think Leavenworth. Two are in Farmington. Armed robbery. My youngest is in juvie. [pause] But my girl is doing great. She's the only straight arrow in the bunch. And I can't take credit for it. My mother raised them all for real. I was rarely home. I wonder how Tiffany turned out the way she did. She won't even look at any drug—street or prescription.

Probably won't take a Tylenol Plus on a bet. Guess she's set her mind to never turn out like her rotten momma.

CHILD CUSTODY GIRL: I'm sorry. I sure hope my girls don't follow in my footsteps. I was wild.

SNARKY GIRL: They will if you don't straighten up yourself and show them what's right. Kids don't listen to what you say. They watch what you do. My boys saw me shooting up and spending big money in my hay-day, boosting days. I guess they don't know anything else.

CHILD CUSTODY GIRL: Yes, Ma'am. [thoughtful pause]

GOSSIP GIRL: Miss Patty, what did Faye do to get here? She doesn't seem like she'd do anything bad?

OLD LIFER: Well, Faye and her husband had a volatile relationship.

CHILD CUSTODY GIRL: What's volatile?

GOSSIP GIRL: Yeah, what's that?

OLD LIFER: Volatile means they had short fuses. She was on anti-depressants because of his abuse, and they both were drinkers. Drugs and alcohol make a lethal combination. They had a big brawl, but that time he pulled a gun, and somehow in the struggle he was the one who ended up dead. It's really so awful for everyone. Bother were regular people—worked at the Ford plant for years. Not criminals. The worst part is she really loved her husband.

CHILD SUPPORT GIRL: Wow. How long has she been locked up?

OLD LIFER: Around 22 years, I believe. I remember when she landed in county jail. A girl at the old prison met her there and told me about her case. That was right after the Great Flood of '93.

CHILD SUPPORT GIRL: If you don't mind me asking, Miss Patty, how long have you been locked up?

OLD LIFER: Over twenty-seven years.

CHILD SUPPORT GIRL: [incredulously] You came in before I was born?

OLD LIFER: Thanks, Bird. That sure makes me feel old. [smile]

CHILD SUPPORT GIRL: When do you get to go home?

OLD LIFER: I will get to see the Parole Board in 23 years, when I'm 86, but they may not let me go then. Who knows? If they don't, I'll beat them down with my cane! [mimes crotchety old lady with cane and chuckles]

CHILD SUPPORT GIRL: That's not funny! I want you to be able to go home to your kids and grandkids. Now.

OLD LIFER: If only you were in charge, Bird, but I refused to take the plea and I'm serving life with no parole for 50 years, so I gotta serve 50 years before I can talk to the parole board. Let that be a lesson. Don't trust a jury. Just because you've been charged with a crime is enough for most people o believe you are guilty. Are these all the papers you have? [Child Custody Girl nods]

PHONE GIRL 2: [on phone] Hello! Hello, baby! Just wanted to wish you a happy birthday! [pause] Yes, I'd love to sing to you! Everyone wants to sing to you, Sierra! [begins song and everyone on stage joins in] Happy Birthday to you, Happy Birthday to you, Happy Birthday, dear Sierra, Happy Birthday to you!

SEVERAL: [sing loudly] And many more—outside the door!

PHONE GIRL 2: Yeah, my friends all know you, Sweetie. I talk about you all the time and make everyone make over your pictures. [pause] Yeah, that's the way we sing it in here. Are you having a good day, sissy? [phone goes dead] What? Hello? Hello? [bangs phone] DAMNATION! THE PHONE CUT OFF! I'M OUT OF MINUTES AND IT'S HER FOURTH BIRTHDAY. I HATE THIS FRIGGIN PLACE! I HATE IT! [exits in a huff]

SNARKY GIRL: [calls behind her] Shoulda budgeted and not wasted your minutes on that man. [to group] You know it's true... I'm just saying...

HUNGRY GIRL: [enters] Lunch sucked. I couldn't eat that slop. [to Snarky Girl] Mickie, do you gotta soup I can have? I'll pay you back, I promise. But not until state pay hits.

SNARKY GIRL: Or never.

HUNGRY GIRL: [dramatically] I'm starving!

OLD LIFER: I gotcha, Jen. Lunch did suck. Don't die just yet. Hang on. [Old Lifer exits to fetch Ramen soup.]

LOUD SPEAKER: LINE UP FOR SMOKE BREAK. LINE UP ON YOUR LEVER. IF YOU LIVE UPSTAIRS, LINE UP UPSTAIRS. LINE UP FOR SMOKE BREAK. NO STRAGGLERS. IF YOU'RE NOT LINED UP, YOU'RE NOT GOING TO SMOKE.

[Old Lifer re-enters with Ramen soup, Hungry Girl reaches for it]

OLD LIFER: Whoa, Jennifer Marie, how long have you been locked up? Don't grab it in front of the camera. I'm going to lay it on the chair, and you sit beside it and scoop it up. When you get up to leave, hold it in front of you so it doesn't show on the camera. Let's be smart about breaking the no-giving rule. OK, Honey? [Hungry Girl does as told and exits, walks offstage and re-enters for smoke break line.]

HUNGRY GIRL: [on way out] Thank you, Miss Patty, but my middle name isn't Marie.

OLD LIFER: I just made that up. Both names get kids' attention even when it's not their names. What is your middle name?

HUNGRY GIRL: [exiting] Ann. Just plain Ann. No E.

OLD LIFER: That's my middle name, too! No E.

HUNGRY GIRL: Thanks again, Miss Patty Ann. You're the best!

SNARKY GIRL: Yeah, the best easy touch.

GOSSIP GIRL: [in smoke break line] Miss Patty, guess who's back. You'll never guess.

OLD LIFER: If I can't possibly guess, Amy, why are you asking?

GOSSIP GIRL: Come on and guess. You'll never guess in a million years.

OLD LIFER: Martha Stewart.

GOSSIP GIRL: No...? [puzzled] I don't know her, do I?

SNARKY GIRL: Shut the front door! Have you been livin' under a rock all your stupid life? You've never heard of Martha Friggin Stewart?

EAR HUSTLE GIRL: She got a contraband violation and it was reported on CNN!

GOSSIP GIRL: [trying to place her] Did she work at clothing issue?

GOSSIP GIRL: NO! Martha Stewart is the most famous female prisoner of all time, that's all. [Gossip Girl flees, so Snarky tells anyone who will listen] She only did a hot minute, though, cause she's rich. You know: Money talks and bullshit walks.

CHILD CUSTODY GIRL: What did they bust her on?

EAR HUSTLE GIRL: It was an egg. Guess she planned to whip up a soufflé in her cell.

CHILD CUSTODY GIRL: [incredulously] She came to prison for stealing an egg?

EAR HUSTLE GIRL: No, that was the contraband violation! Mick, what did she fall on?

SNARKY GIRL: Uh, some kind of insider trading or some other kinda Wall Street crap.

SNARKY GIRL: What is that? An inside job?

SNARKY GIRL: No... [stammers because she doesn't really know] Well, uh, it doesn't matter. It's called white-collar crime, the kind rich, smart people commit, so you'll never have to worry about it.

CHILD CUSTODY GIRL: You said everyone should know about her... [Snarky ignored her and concentrates on her yarn]

QUESTION GIRL: [enters with workbook and pencil and interrupts] What's seven times five?

SEVERL: Thirty-five.

QUESTION GIRL: Are you sure?

ALL: YES!

PAROLE GIRL: [interrupts with face sheet] If you have two sevens running wild, how much time will you serve?

SNARKY GIRL: Do I look like a friggin parole officer to you? [chaining furiously]

OLD LIFER: What did your IPO tell you?

PAROLE GIRL: Not what I wanted to hear?

SMOKER 1: If they transfer me, I'll never see my mom and kids again.

SMOKER 2: In '98 when I was there, my grandma never visited. She couldn't afford the gas. Chilli's is clean across the state.

PAROLE GIRL: [to smoker] If you have four sevens and have been down twice... or maybe three times, how much time will you have to do this time?

SMOKER MOOCH: Got a spare roll-your-own? I'll pay you back...

ACT IV:

LOUD SPEAKER: SMOKE BREAK. QUIET IN THE ROTUNDA. NO STRAGGKERS. SMOKE BREAK. QUIETLY. [Girls exit like usual. Phone Girl 3 gets on phone and mimes calling, waiting and talking.]

GOSSIP GIRL: [leaving for smoke break hollering behind her] Marty Jones is back. 'Member? She used to mess with Lil Dog? Back on a technical... she says. Never thought I'd see her again. I'll tell you more later...

OLD LIFER: [to herself] At least she's alive. So many of these girls OD.

SNARKY GIRL: [to herself] I can't say one word about Marty. This is my seventh "tour of duty".

CHILD CUSTODY GIRL: Wow! I'm never coming back! Ever.

SNARKY GIRL: Everybody says that... Nobody plans to come to prison, trust me!

OLD LIFER: [to Snarky Girl] Have you chained 12 yet? What? I said 12 not 1200! Rip it out.

SNARKY GIRL: Again?

OLD LIFER: Yes. 12. Just 12. You're making a potholder, not an afghan.

SNARKY GIRL: I gotta go smoke!

CHILD CUSTODY GIRL: Thought you quit.

SNARKY GIRL: [hollers behind her as she exits] I've quit a lot!

LATE GIRL: [pulling on coat] WAIT, DON'T LET THE DOOR CLOSE! WAIT! HEY!

OLD LIFER: [as Late Girl rushes by] Hey, Glennis, why are you always late?

LATE GIRL: [indignantly] Why would you say that? I'm not always late. [rushes out hollering] DON'T LET THAT DOOR CLOSE! WAIT! HEY!

LOUD SPEAKER: ICE DETAIL ON A-WING. ICE DETAIL ON A-WING.

OLD LIFER: Does anyone wanna go with me to get ice? [grabs cooler off stage and crosses off.]

CHILD CUSTODY GIRL: I gotcha back, Miss Patty.
[exit together]

 PHONE GIRL 3: [loudly] Are friggin kidding me?
You're pregnant? I thought you were... ya know, using
protection... [pause] No, baby, I'm not mad. I, I'm just
surprised. Do you know who the daddy is? [pause] Uh,
no, I don't know him. [pause] I'm just not ready to be a
grandma yet. Yeah, I was 14 when I had you, honey, but I
hoped you'd... that you'd... [a girl comes up and mimes
that she wants the phone next] [loud and threatening]
BACK OFF, BITCH! I'M CONVERSATIN' HERE.
TAKE THAT FIFTEEN MINUTE LIMIT AND
SHOVE IT UP YOUR BIG FAT ASS! THIS IS AN
IMPORTANT CALL! [interrupting girl sits at table mad]
[Phone Girl into phone] Oh, nothing. That was nothing.
Yeah, Baby, I am happy for you. A baby is always a
blessing. [While action continues, she mimes
conversation with head down for privacy then hangs up
and slides off stage thoughtfully]

LOUD SPEAKER: ICE DETAIL ICE DETAIL ON A-
WING.
COSMO GIRL: [coming back from smoke break] That's
why I'm taking cosmo. I need to settle down and think of
my future. I don't wanna spend my life comin' in and out
a here. I need a skill, a way to make a livin' for me and
my kids. I like messin' with hair...

EAR HUSTLE GIRL 1: That one counselor in treatment
told me that there won't be any change in my life unless I
make a change.

EAR HUSTLE GIRL 2: [seriously] That's deep. Really
deep.

SNARKY GIRL: [back form smoke break and back to table] Yeah, deep like I need my state boots on to get around in bullshit this deep... or hip waders...

COUGHER GIRL: [enters and crosses choking] I gotta quit.

LOUD SPEAKER: LAST CALL FOR ICE DETAIL. LAST CALL FOR ICE.

ALL: [angry to rotunda] THEY WENT ALREADY!

GOSSIP GIRL: Mickie, is it true that we had a cannibal here?

SNARKY GIRL: Well, that's what she said.

GOSSIP GIRL: She ate people?

SNARKY GIRL: Didn't I just say that? They don't call em cannibals cause they eat cantaloupe! She said black people tasted like chicken, and white people tasted like cheese.

GOSSIP GIRL: You're full of crap! [sits down]

[Old Lifer and Child Custody Girl enter with cooler, set it down.]

OLD LIFER: [to Snarky Girl] Mick, rip it out, then chain 12. We can't go on until you chain 12.

SNARKY GIRL: I'm not cut out for this. [throws yarn down and limps to exit] My leg hurts. Really bad. I gotta go lay down. [exits]

GOSSIP GIRL: Miss Patty, did there used to be a cannibal here?

OLD LIFER: Well, that's what she told me, but who knows. Vicky was a character, but I never saw her "chow down" on anybody.

EAR HUSTLE GIRLS: Ohhh! Ew!

GOSSIP GIRL: Wow.

OLD LIFER: It'd sure give you pause if she told you she was having some "Chinese" for dinner or "a little Italian". [everyone laughs]

EAR HUSTLE GIRL: I heard that they pulled her teeth out so she wouldn't eat anybody.

OLD LIFER: That's a bunch of hogwash! Prison lore. But as I recall, she only had one tooth in the front [demonstrates]. We called it the "can opener". [girls laugh]

GOSSIP GIRL: What did she look like?

OLD LIFER: She's a cross between W.C. Fields and Alf. [some girls laugh and agree]

SOME: "Exactly!" "What a perfect description!"

GOSSIP GIRL: Who's W. C. Fields?

OLD LIFER; Oh, my gosh1 You've never heard of W. C. Fields? [impersonation:] "Ya bother me, kid." [Gossip Girl shakes her head] [heavy sigh] I'm a fossil, a dinosaur!

QUESTION GIRL: [with notebook] How do you spell interrogate?

OLD LIFER: I-N-T-E-R-R-O-G-A-T-E

QUESTION GIRL: Slow down!

OLD LIFER: [slowly] I-N-T, E-R-R, O. Then gate: G-A-T-E.

QUESTION GIRL: Are you sure? It doesn't look right.

OLD LIFER: Look it up. I have a dictionary.

QUESTION GIRL: How can I find it, if I can't spell it?

EAR HUSTLE GIRL: She has a point.

OLD LIFER: [Turns to Bird, who looks lost.] Bird, don't fret. I'll write a letter for you to sign. I've done it before. Hopefully they'll knock down your payments to something you can live with or defer debt until you parole. Don't look so doubtful. I guarantee we'll fix this. OK?

CHILD CUSTODY GIRL: Thank you so much, Miss Patty. I wanna see my girls when I get out. [dreamy] Marlie is seven, a tomboy just like me. Allison is prissy, a little princess all in punk, She's just three. And tiny for her age.

OLD LIFER: My Carrie was little bitty for her age, too. And smart as a whip. She was just ten when I had to leave her. She's almost 38 now.

CHILD CUSTODY GIRL: [hand to heart, nearly in tears] I miss my girls so much, my head hearts. [everyone becomes quiet, thinking of their own kids]

ACT V:

LOUD SPEAKER: FIRE DRILL. FIRE DRILL! EXIT THE BUILDING! EVERYBODY OUT! [Everyone springs into action. Everything from now on is hectic and fast.]

OLD LIFER: I gotta grab my coat. Bird! Get yours. Fast.

CHILD CUSTODY GIRL: Should I leave the letters out? No, I'd better take them back.

OLD LIFER: Come on, Bird1 Scoop up those letters. Hurry!

GRUMBLE GIRL 1: It's freezing out there!

GRUMBLE GIRL 2: Is this a real fire drill? There's no alarm. Did you hear an alarm?

LOUD SPEAKER: DO NOT STOP AT THE BATHROOM. GET OUT NOW! FIRE DRILL!
[a girl stops dead in tracks at edge of bathroom and detours to exit]

GRUMBLE GIRL 3: JUDY'S IN THE SHOWER! [As most speak, they exit off stage except for Shower Girl 2, offstage, who must wait for her clothes.]

SHOWER GIRL 2: [hollering offstage] GET MY COAT AND SHOE. SOMEONE! PEACHES! ANYONE IN

204! I CAN"T GO BACK TO MY ROOM! HELP! [girl shows up with coat and boots]

GRUMBLE GIRL 4: Is it sleeting out there? Or snowing?

COUGHER GIRL: [coughs out] I gotta quit.

GRUMBLE GIRL 5: GET YOUR ASS IN GEAR!

GOSSIP GIRL: At least now I'll get the scoop from CoCo 'bout why Heather got that violation.

GRUMBLE GIRL 4: It is sleeting! This is cruel and unusual punishment!

SNARKY GIRL 2: It's not that unusual...

SHOWER GIRL 2: I STILL GOT SHAMPOO IN MY HAIR AND AM ALL SOAPED UP. I HATE THIS! [gets coat and boots] YOU COULDN'T A GRABBED MY SOCKS? GEEZ... THEY WAS IN MY BOOTS! [hobbles out pulling on boots]

LOUD SPEAKER: FIRE DRILL! QUIET IN THE ROTUNDA. SINGLE FILE. LINE UP IN SINGLE FILE.

GRUMBLE GIRL 6: [rubbing eyes, indignant] CAN"T A LADY TAKE A NAP AROUND HERE? THEY'RE DISRESPECTING US WITH THIS STUPID FIRE DRILL ON OUR DAY OFF! I HATE THIS PLACE! [everyone exits]

LATE GIRL: [pulling on coat] WAIT! HEY! DON'T LET THAT DOOR CLOSE! WAIT FOR ME!

PHOTOGRAPHY

Window
Mark Ehlrichmann

229

Risky
Aimee Manjarres

Windows From Prison

Brief description of project:
Mark Strandquist, Windows From Prison Coordinator

Windows From Prison features creative exchanges that
connect prisoners to their past, and fosters space and
humanistic entry points for students, NGO's, family
members of prisoners, policy makers, former prisoners
and many others to engage with the sources, impacts, and
alternatives to incarceration. During a series of
workshops, prisoners are invited to choose, "If you had a
window in your cell, what place from your past would it
look out to?" Participants provide a detailed memory
from the chosen location and describe how they would
want the photograph composed. The locations are then
photographed and an image is handed or mailed back to
the corresponding prisoners. Utilizing collaborative
practice, interactive installations, and public interventions,
the project facilitates a discursive space for crisis level
issues concerning incarceration and for the civic and
artistic ways in which we engage the world.

When the project is exhibited, the images and
corresponding writing become the starting point for
additional actions that engage communities in
collaboration, dialogue, and exchange. Corresponding
programing has included poetry from prison, film
screenings, letter writing workshops, a lending library,
teach-ins led by community members affected by
incarceration, workshops on restorative justice, and many
others. Each exhibit features a newspaper including
information on the project, a schedule of public events,
additional photo requests for readers to fulfill, and
information/editorials written by local groups working on
issues around incarceration and re-entry. Newspapers are

placed across the surrounding region in bright orange
newspaper boxes.

When exhibited the size of photographs presented to the
public is consistent with the restrictions imposed on
pictures sent to prisons.

I was absconded for forty days from drug court. I was staying with my then sponsor Gary, who allowed me to set-up living quarters in his garage. While there I did repairs and cleaning, also scraping and painting the exterior of his house. At the same time I was developing a routine that was displaying some positive results on the surface, I was only creating a more stressful climate the longer I delayed turning myself in. It was the elephant in the room—everywhere I went—at moms, Garys, various friends dads.

I began to go for walks at Bryan Park and discovered a spot of Serenity. Its past the soccer fields beside a man-made pond with a stone border. There is a bench, wooden. Its under a weeping willow. This is where I 'sorted it out.'

I was absconded for forty days from drug court. I was staying with my then sponsor Gary, who allowed me to set up living quarters in his garage. While there I did repairs and cleaning, also scraping and painting the exterior of his house. At the same time I was developing a routine that

was displaying some positive results on the surface, I was
only creating a more stressful climate the longer I delayed
turning myself in. It was the elephant in the room—
everywhere I went—at mom's, Gary's, various friends'
pads.

I began to go for walks at Bryan Park and discovered a
spot of serenity. It's past the soccer fields beside a man-
made pond with a stone border. There is a bench,
wooden. It's under a weeping willow. This is where I
"sorted it out."

I layed down across the rocks and took a long deep
breath in and out. The mid-summer sun was slowly
absorbed, photosynthesized into an unconscious smile
across my face. Around me the dogs ran, barked, jumped,
chased, snarled, dug and splashed. The water burbling
just behind. Fresh air rushes in and gentle confidence
rolls out.

-Danny

I'm staring at a place where I once was a child. A
confused little boy in search of some type of purpose, in
search of some type of meaning. 7 years of age in an
urban apartment complex w/ no parental direction.
Having to sponge everything from the neighborhood of
sex, money, deception, manipulation, violence, & drugs.
But still would rather be out there than inside my
household of physical abuse & neglect where a mother

worked all day, leaving me in the care of a father who abused the use of crack cocaine & a short fused temper. I find myself alone to an empty house when I awake in the morning but actually relieved that my father was not there. This is a place in my past that dictated my current events. I became a product of my environment. A participant in the game of activities of my old neighborhood....sex money, deception, manipulation, violence, & Drugs.

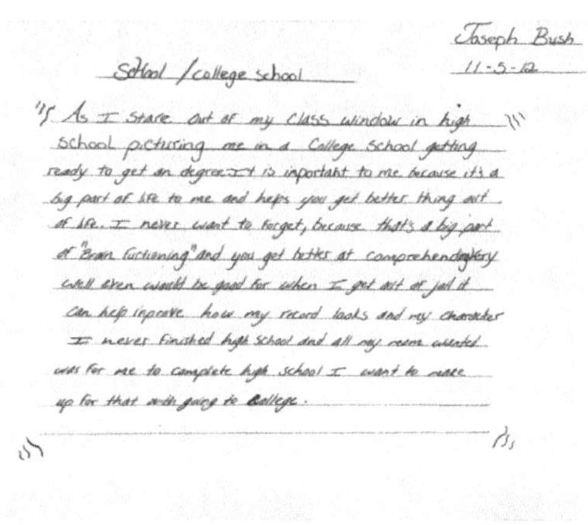

School/ college school.

As I stare out of my class window in high school picturing me in a college school getting ready to get an degree. It is important to me because it's a big part of life to me and helps you get better thing out of life. I never want to forget, because that's a big part of "Brain functioning" and you get better at comprehending very well even would be good for when I get out of jail it can help improve how my record looks and my character I never finished high school and all my mom wanted was for me to complete high school I want to make up for that with going to college.

The place I am living in now is dark & glooming and feels
like hell. I feel like I am losing my mind, but the only
thing that keeps me sane, is my little window. Every time I
feel the walls closing in on me I stare out my window, and
it's like a breath of fresh air, because right outside my
window is my mom's house and it's so big bright and
beautiful. I spent some of the best years of my life in this
house, every time I look at this house it brings me hope
and joy in some of my roughest times. Like my mom's

driveway so big and neat, surrounded by gravel, I went
from learning to walk out there, to rock fights out there,
to learning how to drive out there, man I miss this place!

(7 1/2 years left)
God Bless

Looking through this window I can see this long hallway. My sister and I running halfway down the hallway and sliding the remaining of the way in out socks. At the age of 12 yrs old are my sister 6 at this time, seeing the world through my innocent eyes. This hallway was a safe haven for us. This hallway is filled with much laughter and fun. No worries.
I miss this place.

About the Editors and Contributors

HANNAH EHLERS (Editor-in-Chief) is thrilled to have worked in partnership with Alexa to edit the 2014 edition of Tacenda—the most inclusive and diverse edition yet. An undergraduate student at American University majoring in Jewish Studies with a German Area Studies minor, Ehlers is a Consulting Editor for BleakHouse Publishing. She is dedicated to social justice and has done extensive work to promote animal welfare, wildlife conservation, Middle East peace, and criminal justice. Ehlers is grateful for Professor Johnson's guidance and support through this challenging and enriching process.

ALEXA MARIE KELLY (Editor-in-Chief) is grateful for the opportunity to work on Tacenda Literary Magazine 2014. She believes in the power of creative writing to remind us that we are human. Her goal in editing this year's Tacenda was to engage diverse authors from every corner of humanity. Kelly works as BleakHouse Publishing's Chief Editorial Officer, affectionately managing submissions. She would like to thank Hannah, Professor Johnson and her coffeemaker, without whom this publication would not have been possible.

ROBERT JOHNSON (Consulting Editor) is a Professor of Justice, Law and Criminology at American University, Editor and Publisher of BleakHouse Publishing, and a widely published and award winning author of books and articles on crime and punishment, including works of social science, law, and fiction. He has testified or testified expert affidavits on capital and other criminal cases in many venues, including US state and federal courts, the U.S. Congress, and the European Commission of Human Rights. He is best known for his book, Death

Work: A Study of the Modern Execution Process, which
won the Outstanding Book Award of the Academy of
Criminal Justice Sciences. Johnson is a Distinguished
Alumnus of the Nelson A. Rockefeller College of Public
Affairs and Policy, University at Albany, State University
of New York.

S. JAMEL BELLAMY (Author) is the pen name for
Stanley S Bellamy. Bellamy is a published author of two
short stories: Prison Songs and Deadly Passion; and
Devotion, his debut urban suspense novel. He is now
seeking a new publishing house willing to publish the
sequel to 'Devotion,' entitled: 'Deadly Devotion.' He had
also written numerous articles and position papers on
parole reform. He is currently housed in Sullivan
Correctional Facility, a New York State prison, serving a
sixty-two to life sentence for a crime committed in
October of 1995.

EMILY BLAU (Author) is an undergraduate student
pursuing a degree in Public Health at American
University in Washington, DC. She is from Long Island,
New York, and is interested in epidemiology and film.

MAGGIE BRENNAN (Author) was raised in
Doylestown, Pennsylvania and is currently studying
Business Administration with a specialization in
Management at American University in Washington,
D.C. She is pursuing a minor in Creative Writing and is
in the process of developing a project to help bring writing
as an outlet to veterans suffering from Post Traumatic
Stress Disorder. Brennan is a former intern at the Travis
Manion Foundation, based in Doylestown, Pennsylvania
and Publicity Coordinator for the School of Public Affairs
Leadership Program at American University. She will be
graduating with the class of 2016.

AMANDA BRENNER (Author) is a sophomore studying International Relations and Systems of Justice at American University.

HAKEEM 7X. BUTLER (Author) is a contributing author to Tacenda Literary Magazine.

EMMY CAIRNS (Author) is a sophomore at American University, majoring in International Relations. She took Deprivation of Liberty with Professor Johnson in order to learn more about the inner workings of the American justice system and the ways in which it can be improved.

ALISHA CARRINGTON (Author) is the Outreach Assistant for Free Minds Book Club & Writing Workshop. At 16, she was charged as an adult and sentenced to seven and a half years in prison. She was housed in the DC Jail with adults in solitary confinement. During her incarceration, she found poetry to be therapeutic as it helped her express herself in a creative way, and allowed her to share her story with others. She wrote the poem "Colors" just months before her release in 2013 to express her desire for change. Now home, she plans to study social work at Montgomery College.

D.C. (Author), 18, is from Washington, DC. He is a member of Free Minds Book Club & Writing Workshop. He received an Honorable Mention in the 2013 Regional Scholastic Writing Awards.

HARMONY DAVIES (Author) holds her B.S. degree in Behavioral Science-Sociology from Utah Valley University. She is currently living in Seattle, WA and is currently collaborating on several pieces regarding issues surrounding capital punishment that are slated for publication. These works include "Utah Resident's Attitudes Toward the Death Penalty" and a chapter in the upcoming edition of America's Experiment with Capital Punishment co-authored with Robert Johnson of American University in Washington D.C.

REV. MARK EHRLICHMANN (Photographer), Deaf Missionary, focuses on Deaf and Special Needs Ministry including Prison Ministry in the Greater Baltimore, MD area since 2007. He is Director of Embracing Lambs Ministries, non-profit organization that provides ministry in a wide variety of needs. He participates in social work, advocacy, pastoral care, counseling, and mentoring. Ehrlichmann is vice-president of Helping Educate to Advance the Rights of the Deaf (HEARD) and has worked with Talila Lewis since meeting her in 2006 on Access issues in the Criminal Justice system.

CASSANDRA FOWLER (Author) is a Frederick Douglass Distinguished Scholar studying Justice and Law at American University's School of Public Affairs. She has worked with community-based organizations in South Africa, and is currently developing an educational program for middle school students in DC. She hopes to go on to law school and use her legal expertise to improve and empower DC communities, and continue to use writing as a means of advocacy.

ERIN GEORGE (Author) is a Consulting Editor for BleakHouse and a life sentence inmate, who has received a PEN Award and a Tacenda Literary Magazine Award, both for poetry. Her first collection of poetry, Origami Heart, was published by BleakHouse Publishing.

G GWIN (Author) was born and raised in Long Beach California. She is currently serving a life sentence at Pelican Bay State Prison for a host of charges and enhancements. Gwin has been writing poetry for about eight years. Her poetry stems from emotional turmoil and hardships. It also stems from observations of people, and from being enlightened by the happenings of the world, country, state, and society. Since she has been incarcerated, she has been able to see things in a different light and become patient and open-minded enough to observe both sides of the coin.

CHARLES HUCKELBURY (Author) has received four PEN awards for fiction and nonfiction and is the author of two books of poetry, Tales from the Purple Penguin and Distant Thunder, both published by BleakHouse. He writes a monthly newsletter for the Prisons Foundation in Washington, D.C.

ARTHUR JOHNSON (Author) is currently incarcerated in FCI Tucson. He is 24 years old, from Washington, DC. He loves to read and write poems. Once he is released he plans to continue his education and study photography. Johnson is a dedicated member of Free Minds Book Club & Writing Workshop.

KAREN LAUSA (Author) is developer and founder of the Words Beyond Bars Project, which introduces transformative literature to prisoners.

EMMA LOBUONO (Author): Instant human – just add coffee. Slowly stir in one degree from American University. Serves the world.

ARTHUR LONGWORTH (Author) is a current prisoner at the Washington State Reformatory in Monroe, Washington. He has won three PEN awards and considerable recognition for his ability to write about prison.

RICK LYON (Author) had his first book of poems, Bell 8, published by BOA Editions. His work has appeared in the Massachusetts Review, the Missouri Review, the Nation and others. He has work forthcoming in the Colorado Review. A boat captain, originally from New England, Lyon now lives and works in Chicago.

MATT MAGARITY (Author) is twenty years old and a sophomore at Franklin and Marshall College. He plays football and writes in his spare time because it is the only way he knows how to make some sense of the world. Magarity is from Willow Grove, PA and attended La Salle College High School. He wrote "Burnt Out" in his frustration with a culture that fosters and encourages negative acts like bullying, as the abusers not only go unpunished but often are socially rewarded for their brutal audacity.

SANDRA MAJESTIC (Author) is a master's student at American University. She studies justice, law, and society while concentrating in jurisprudence and social thought. Since day one at American University, her main focus has been on many different human rights issues. She has argued about reproductive rights, expressed ideas on the equality of education, and researched many different genocides. While in class with Professor Robert Johnson, she developed an inspiring interest into the lives of convicts. She currently interns for the ACLU of the Nation's Capital, which she hopes one day leads to an employment opportunity as an advocate for their prison project program.

TONY MALINAUKAS (Author) is a literature major at American University and an award-winning BleakHouse Publishing author.

AIMEE MANJARRES (Photographer) is a second year student at American University. She is a communication studies major with a minor in sociology. This semester she will be interning in the communications department for Free the Slaves. Her recent trip to South Africa with American University Alternative Break has sparked an interest in studying minority inequalities and has influenced many of her writing pieces.

DANIEL MARKS (Author) is a Frederick Douglass Distinguished Scholar and a University Honors Program student at American University. He enjoys volunteering with diverse, under-resourced communities and also enjoys participating in scientific research. In his spare time, Marks writes free-verse poetry.

CARLA MAVADDAT (Cover Design) is an undergraduate majoring in Political Science at McGill University with a passion for photography and design. Mavaddat is interested in human rights and social justice, and tries to incorporate that in her work. Her photos have appeared in *Adore Noir,* among other venues. She is the graphics and design editor for *BleakHouse Review,* Art Curator for BleakHouse Publishing, and a Victor Hassine Memorial Scholar.

BETTY MAY (Author) is a wife, mother, theatrical director, playwright, novelist, teacher, and clown. She has directed productions in schools, community centers, dinner theaters, and in her own theater. Her career has taken her to Europe, where she toured with a teen company; to Central America, where she directed shows with street kids; and to a women's prison, where, with a group of lifers, she developed a play: FACES, that allowed the women's voices to be heard. The latter led to an exciting opportunity to compose and direct a show: FROM PRISON TO STAGE, at Washington D.C.'s Kennedy Center.

MOLLY MCGINNIS (Author) is a student at American
University in Washington, D.C. She has been published
in Cicada Magazine, Thexe Adroit Journal, Crashtest,
The Sierra Nevada Review, and has work forthcoming in
Cleaver Magazine. Molly is also a two-time winner of a
national American Voices Medal through the 2012 and
2013 Scholastic Art and Writing Awards. Despite this,
she is actually horrible at telling stories in real life and
would much rather chug coffee and listen to yours.

CHAVEZ MYERS (Author) is an 18-year-old writer from
Washington, D.C. He is a Sunni Muslim who is currently
incarcerated in the D.C. Jail awaiting a 30-year sentence.
He lives by one moral: "remaining loyal." Loyalty to his
religion, to his family, and to himself is what keeps him
going. He is a dedicated member of Free Minds Book
Club & Writing Workshop and loves the positive things
they do for people around the city.

SUSAN NAGELSEN (Author) is the director of the
writing program at New England College in Henniker,
NH. Her book, Exiled Voices: Portals of Discovery, is a
collection of writings by women and men in prisons
across the country. She is associate editor of the Journal
of Prisoners on Prisons, a peer-reviewed criminal justice
journal published by the University of Ottawa. Her most
recent work appears in the New Plains Review and
Ephipanymag.org.

ZOÉ ORFANOS (Author) is in her last year as an
Honors undergraduate at American University in
Washington D.C, after spending a year studying
Literature and International Human Rights at Oxford
University. Working toward a Bachelors degree in Law
and Society with minors in Creative Writing and
Literature, Orfanos graduates in May of 2014 from the
School of Public Affairs. Orfanos has achieved both Best

Short Story and Best Poem for her contributions to The BleakHouse Review. Orfanos served as the 2012 Editor-in-Chief of Tacenda Literary Magazine. Throughout her education, Orfanos has dedicated both time and energy to studying and experiencing the realities of social justice. Having recently volunteered and interned at Offender Aid & Restoration in Arlington, Virginia, Orfanos is now volunteering as a writing teacher in the Montgomery County Correctional Facility in Maryland.

PATRICIA PREWITT (Author), grandmother of ten, was raised on a Missouri Ranch. In 1984 her husband was murdered, she turned down a plea agreement and was convicted to serve life without no parole for 50 years. She's earned an AA degree and Personal Fitness Trainer's certification from AFAA. She is a computer programmer for the DOC, a member of Prison Performing Arts, won a 2006 Pen writing award, and is included in the 2013 anthology *Too Cruel, Not Unusual Enough* by the Other Death Penalty Project. The Georgetown Law's Community Justice Project seeks executive clemency on her behalf.

KRISTEN PULKSTENIS (Author) is an undergraduate in the honors program at American University majoring in Law and Society and pursuing a minor and translation certification in Spanish. A previously published poet, she takes special interest in issues of juvenile crime, community participation in the justice system, and disability in prison. She believes these experiences can be made accessible through creative writing. Originally from New Jersey, she enjoys volunteering and working with animals in her spare time. Pulkstenis looks forward to earning a law degree after graduation and to a career in criminal litigation.

MIKALA REMPE (Author) is a freshman studying literature and creative writing at American University. Her genre of choice is poetry; especially slam or spoken word poetry. She has a growing interest in prison reform.

VALERIE RENNOLL (Author) grew up in the small town of Glen Rock, Pennsylvania. She studies audio technology and physics at American University. She enjoys using poetry as an outlet to explore the criminal justice system.

WILLIAM ROTH (Author) is currently a professor at Kutztown University. Two of his short stories have been placed in national competitions—Serpentinia and New Millennium Writing. He has also published stories in The McGuffin, The Schuykill Valley Journal, Overtime, and Tacenda Literary Magazine. His first novel was called "The Pelican and the Pearl and the Live Oak Tree."

ANNE SCHERER (Author) is a writer and artist who resides in Rochester, Minnesota. She has been a long time advocate for Peace and Justice issues and currently is pursuing advocacy work with Victims of Abuse. Anne enjoys reading, music, walking and of course writing and drawing. Anne graduated from the University of Wisconsin -Madison with a Bachelors degree in Art with her focus on Drawing and Photography.

MARK STRANDQUIST (Contributor) is an artist, educator, and organizer. His projects facilitate interactions that incorporate viewers as direct participants and present alternative models for the civic and artistic ways in which we engage the world around us. Each interactive installation he facilitates functions not as a culmination but as a catalyst for dialogue, exchange, and community action. He is currently an adjunct faculty at the Corcoran College of Art and the Virginia Museum of Fine Arts.

SONIA TABRIZ (Text Design) is a merit scholar and
J.D. candidate at The George Washington University Law
School, where she is Editor-In-Chief of the Public
Contract Law Journal. Tabriz graduated with honors and
summa cum laude from American University with majors
in both Law & Society and Psychology. She received the
Outstanding Scholarship at the Undergraduate Level
award from American University for her award-winning
works of fiction, legal commentaries, artwork,
presentations, university-wide accolades, and academic
achievement. Tabriz is the Managing Editor of
BleakHouse Publishing.

STEPHANIE VELA (Author) is a student at American
University majoring in sociology. She is originally from
southern California. She hopes to use her passion for
social work and education to make an impact on the
marginalized of society.